Phyllis

Isabelle Howe

Phyllis

Olympia Publishers
London

www.olympiapublishers.com
OLYMPIA PAPERBACK EDITION

A CIP catalogue record for this title is
available from the British Library.

ISBN: 978-1-78830-958-5

This is a work of fiction.
Names, characters, places and incidents originate from the writer's
imagination. Any resemblance to actual persons, living or dead, is
purely coincidental.

First Published in 2021

Olympia Publishers
Tallis House
2 Tallis Street
London
EC4Y 0AB

Printed in Great Britain

Dedication

To my family, my inspiration and the loves of my life.

Also, I dedicate this book to my dear cousin Bill (William Inglis Howe) 1935–2021 Loving father and husband.

Acknowledgements

Thanks again, looking forward to the next.

It was 12th April 1929, Phyllis was twenty-two years old, she was getting married in an hour, she missed her parents already, they were gearing up to move from Fort William, where she had lived most of her life, thousands of miles away to England, and were not attending the wedding. For the first time in her life, she was utterly alone, even her sister Kitty, who was her constant companion growing up, was moving with her parents and her six other siblings. New Delhi was a long way from home.

Phyllis was born and brought up in the British colony of West Bengal India, with her father who was a magistrate and her mother, she had two brothers and four sisters, they had a very happy and comfortable life, their parents were very kind and loving. Now she was to be married to a man who was as old as her mother and will have to live with him in Multan hundreds of miles away from her family. The house he had bought for them to live in was lovely, with many lavish rooms and a small garden, she would have servants to help her with the upkeep, as her new husband was away all the time, he travelled around the country as the district commissioner to West Bengal.

Phyllis was constantly alone after the marriage, and was consoled only by the overseas club and the impending birth of her first child. She missed her family, they had always been there, she loved the little ones and her older brother and sister were her closest confidants. The loneliness was unbearable, although she threw herself into the club, and socializing with the wives of the English gentry including the Viceroy and his wife. She rubbed shoulders with Princes and Maharajas, Russian diplomats, and budding actresses, she taught Sylvia Coleridge how to play tennis and how to horseback ride in Simla, Phyllis recalled how she was so pretty and sung like a lark. Sylvia's mother on the committee with Phyllis and took the overseas club very seriously.

The time was here, at last and as usual, her husband was away, Phyllis gave birth to her first child, a daughter. She was overjoyed, at last she had someone who needed her, this tiny person was dependent on her, the love she felt was overwhelming, but the joy Phyllis felt was short-lived, her husband returned from his trip and was underwhelmed by the new arrival and ordered the servants to take the child, "A daughter, you gave me a daughter? We will have to try again to have a son, I have no use for girls," he said stiffly. Phyllis was destroyed, and as soon as he went out, she retrieved her daughter from the servants and wept bitterly, as she held her child close to her body, "Don't worry my little Meg, I love you," she said.

Phyllis needed her mother more than ever now. Her mother had just given birth herself, less than a month ago, to a baby boy, Richard, so she couldn't travel and her father was busy winding down his job, ready for the move; her older sister was busy with her own children, and her brother had gone to Canada with his career. The year that followed went by slowly as Phyllis kept herself busy with the club and her daughter, her husband only visited her room when he needed the comfort of her bed.

1931. Her parents had gone, Phyllis was totally alone she could only console herself with letter writing — this was less than ideal, and she knew she wouldn't see them for years. They would be staying at her Uncle Rivers' house for a few weeks, then they would be visiting Errol in Canada and finally back to England to secure a residence, her younger siblings were at boarding school in Bengal and her sister Kitty took care of them in the holidays as their parents were traveling with the youngest child.

In July 1931 Phyllis fell for her second child. This time she hoped for a son as maybe her husband would be happy and stay home more often, as he hadn't changed his opinion of his daughter — she was nothing to him. Sure enough in April 1932 she gave birth to a son, her husband looked at the child admiringly, "Yes that's better," he said, he didn't pick up the infant he just left the bedroom where Phyllis lay swaddling her son, Still, things didn't change, he was rarely home and didn't take much interest in his children, in fact as the children grew they were terribly afraid of their father, and hid behind their mother and wept, every time he visited the nursery, Percy was a stern man he had no time for sentiment. Towards his wife he was cold and distant. Phyllis wrote to her parents often telling how cold he was, and she didn't understand why he had married her? He was so different from her father who was a firm family man to her three brothers and four sisters, she missed them more than ever and wished they had not gone to England. Her parents had just purchased a house in Surrey and were ready for the family to reside there, they had sent for the other children as soon as they moved in. her mother wrote often telling her of the weather and how her youngest son was growing, the boarding schools that she was sending her youngest daughter to, and how green England was but it rained a lot she said. She had her hands full acclimatising to the British weather, and she had no housemaids to help her run her large house they had bought in Sanderstead. Her younger sisters were a great help and didn't find it difficult to find jobs as they had a higher quality of education than most and her younger brother was going to a teachers college. She also wrote about how her sister Kitty, who was married to their cousin Mervyn, her mother's sister Lilly's son, and had three children, Kathy, Robert and Patrick, had moved to England and had moved into a very nice neighbourhood quite close by. Her eldest brother Errol and his wife Jessie had just had a second son, they had moved to Canada for a few years then they moved back to Scotland and were staying with Jessie's parents.

Phyllis couldn't help thinking she had made a mistake thinking she could be happy with her husband; he didn't seem interested in her as a woman or as anything really.

Before they were married, he made her feel like she was the most important thing in his life, yes, she knew he was going to be away a lot as he had to travel all over the country as the district commissioner. Still, when he was at home, he only visited her room at night when he wanted to visit her bed. During the day he would be in his study working and had his meals served to him on a tray, or he went out to dinner with his friends from the Himalayan Brotherhood Lodge. Phyllis only got to go when he wanted to show her off to his friends, there was a strict no-women rule unless they had a function. He paid almost no attention to their children, sometimes she thought that was a good thing, as he scared them half to death, she often wondered why he was so cold, had he always been that way, and she didn't see it?

It was the summer season, and the temperature was rising it was time to go to the mountains, Phyllis had an invitation to the Rajah's Palace for the summer, she packed her children up and took the car and driver to Kashmir. It was a long tiring journey and was very hot in the car. For most of the trip, the windows had to be shut as it was getting dusty and the insects were such a pest, but as soon as they arrived in the area, the scenery was lush woodlands and farmlands. Phyllis loved Kashmir, the aroma of saffron growing in the fields, and the fields of maise and wheat and the yellow flowers of the potato fields was so beautiful. She could open the windows and let the soft air blow through the car.

The children were asleep when they arrived, so Phyllis took them straight to bed, the luxurious bedroom that she always stayed in at the palace was so colourful with deep red throws and pillows with gold accents. The ayah slept on a mattress on the floor next to the children's beds, it was an honour to go with the memsahib to the palace for the summer, and the servants often fought for the opportunity to go. Phyllis made them take turns, mostly so everyone had a chance of going, though she did have her favourites, it was extremely important to her that her children were cared for in the kindest manner. This ayah was particularly kind, this was why she was chosen. Phyllis was a constant visitor to the palace, she enjoyed the long walks along the river banks and horseback riding, she loved to play tennis with the other guests. She hated to hear the stories of the tigers they had shot. She knew it was a danger but they were such majestic beasts it was a shame to hear of their demise. She was glad that her husband was too busy to go this year, as she could relax more when he wasn't around, he was so stern and rigid in his views of how a wife should behave and she was getting bored of his Victorian ways, it was the nineteen thirties after all.

It was so lovely to see her children run and play with the other children, it made a change to see them smile and relax, although Meg was frightened of everyone, especially men, all they had to say was hello to her and she wept calling for her mother. Phyllis was worried about her, if she couldn't stop being so scared of everything how was she going to cope when she started school and it was very common for the British children to go to boarding school at five or six years of age. Meg was almost four, the summer was coming to an end and it was nearly time for them to return to New Delhi to the dusty streets and noise. Phyllis packed up her belongings and said her profound thank yous for the invitation to the Maharaja. He was happy to have had her and her beautiful children, and he would be grateful of her presence the following year, as she was well thought of by his other guests in particular the Russian diplomats enjoyed her captivating conversation, and his wives liked the way she treated them, telling them all the stories of British gentry and the British history. They particularly liked the tales she told of love and courage of the kings and queens of England, she told stories to the children, the rhymes and poetry were particular favourites of the royal children, she read to them before they retired to bed almost every night. Phyllis had painted some very nice pictures of the countryside and some of the children and gave them as gifts to the Maharaja just before they left for the long journey back home.

As usual, Percy was nowhere to be seen when they arrived home, and he knew they were due back from the mountains, were they so invisible to him? It was four days before he arrived home, "Oh there you are," he said, looking down his nose at her.

Phyllis exploded at him, "Here we are, yes," she said, "we arrived home and where was our wonderful husband and father? Nowhere that's where!" she screamed.

"If you are going to be hysterical, I'll go to the club. One thing I hate is hysterical women," he said.

"Oh no you won't," she shouted. Phyllis couldn't believe she was saying this. "We have been away for weeks and not a letter, not a phone call from you, Percy. Why am I married to you? Please remind me!" She said "I'm so sick of your coldness towards us, are we nothing to you?" she said.

"Of course you are," he said, quite shocked that she dared

speak to him in this manner, "you have a good life here, you want for nothing," he said.

"There is more to life than to have things," she said close to tears, "you are cold to me. I don't exist unless you are visiting my bed. I want a husband who cares about me and is kind, and you are none of those things. You hate your children, why are we even here?" She looked at him, his face was twisted and red, "Because madam, you are my wife and those are my children," he shouted, "and you will be silent immediately."

"Or what?" she shouted back, "you'll ignore us? You already do, I've never met such a bore as you Percy. The servants get more attention than I do. I'm sick of it, sick to death!" she shouted and left the room.

He strode after her grabbing her wrist. "I have not dismissed you, do not walk away from me!" he screamed. Phyllis tried to loosen her wrist from his grasp, but he was much stronger than she was

"You're hurting me Percy, let me go!"

"You will do as I say Phyllis, or I'll put you out on the street where you belong," he said with venom in his voice. She was stunned, his eyes showed her nothing but hate. No one had ever spoken to him like that before and he wasn't going to let her do it again.

She backed down, "I'm sorry," she said "may I go?"

"Yes, to your room. Do not see to the children tonight they will dine with me, and you will eat with the servants," he said looking at her like she was soil on his shoes.

She looked at him in horror, "Why? You never eat with the children, you will frighten them," she said.

"Don't be ridiculous I am their father, and they will be dining with me, you are excused," he said turning to go back to the drawing room. Phyllis ran to the nursery and shut the door behind her.

The children had just had their bath, ready to dine. They ran to their mother smiling, she hugged them close to her and spoke softly. "Now darlings, your father has asked you to eat with him tonight," she said.

They looked in horror at her, "I don't want to eat with father, mother." Megan said.

"Now darling there is nothing to be frightened of. He has decided, there is nothing to be done, please behave."

Megan started to cry, "Are you eating with us too mother?" she said,

"No, I'm afraid not, I'm not feeling too well, I'm just going to retire early. You need to stop that crying, you know he hates it when you cry," she said.

"Yes mother," Megan said trying to pull herself together.

The table was silent as the children were served their food. Percy was at the far end of the table, luckily, he didn't notice Megan shaking. He looked down the table at the tiny children, "Trip good?" he enquired.

"Yes, quite," Megan replied.

"Looking forward to school?" he said.

"Yes," Megan said, she was lying she hated the idea of going to a strange place and not seeing her mother for months on end, but she knew not to mention a word about it to her father as he lost his temper very quickly, especially with her. Owen, her little brother, was moving things about on his plate, he hated this type of curry, it was far too hot for him.

"Eat up boy!" Percy said sternly.

"It's hot," Owen said and when Percy looked away Megan took some on her plate and winked at the small boy.

"It'll grow hairs on your chest," his father said not looking at them at all

"Yes, Father," Owen said, pretending to eat. "I don't want hairs on my chest," he whispered to Megan. She smiled and took some bread and gave it to her brother so he wouldn't be hungry later, and gave him some of her potatoes as she took the rest of the curry from his plate. Percy was none the wiser as he was too busy eating his food and reading some papers.

"Is there dessert father?" Megan said hopefully.

"Why on earth do you need dessert child!" he shouted. "No doubt that's your mothers idea of spoiling you. If you have finished you may be excused."

The children left the dining room silently. Phyllis was waiting in the hall. She was relieved to see the children were not crying and she had arranged for some dessert in the nursery as she knew Percy wouldn't allow them to have any.

"I'm so proud of you," she said. Hugging her children close to her,

"Oh, Mother, he gave Owen that awful hot curry he doesn't like, do you think he does that on purpose?" Megan said.

"I don't know," she said hugging her children, "but you managed to eat it, you clever boy."

Owen confessed "Meggy ate it when he wasn't looking, and gave me her potatoes and bread."

Phyllis hugged Meg again, "You are the best sister in the world, did you know that darling?" she said. After the children had eaten the dessert, they got washed and ready for bed, Phyllis read them a story, and they fell asleep. Phyllis was miserable, she wanted to see her mother and tell her what he had done. Still, she had gone, it was too far to travel to England.

Later, she entered the drawing-room where Percy was listening to the radio. He ignored her, she cleared her throat and he looked up at her, she started to speak, "I want to visit my parents for Christmas, I know you are busy, but I can take the children and be back by the New Year," she said.

"Not this year," he said, not looking at her, "you are expected to be at the Christmas ball in Simla, and you are committed to that," he said stiffly.

"Well can we go after the ball then?" she asked.

"Not this year, maybe next year," he went back to listening to the radio and waved his hand as though waving her away like one of the servants.

"You said that last year Percy please, I need to see my family."

He glared at her, "Your family, madam, are the people in this house, you had better get used to that." Again he gestured for her to leave.

She left the room, all the time thinking about how she could go, then she remembered he was away through April and May. She could go and be back before he returned and he would never know. The next day she went to the booking office. She looked at the sailing schedules hesitating she took a deep breath and told herself to be brave. She booked herself and the children on the ship *Tuscania* leaving from Bombay and arriving in Liverpool on 30th April 1935. Phyllis was passenger number ninety-nine, Megan was one hundred and Owen was one hundred and one., Clutching her tickets, she returned home and hid the tickets in a secret compartment in the desk that her father had bought her as a wedding gift. She sat at the desk and wrote to her father telling him of her plans. A few weeks later she received a letter back from her him telling her not to be so foolish, he knew her husband's reputation for being over-bearing there's no knowing what his reaction would be if she did this behind his back. Her father wasn't happy when his wife had set their daughter up to marry this man. He had a pretty good idea what her life was like and was helpless to help. If she hadn't had children, he would have said to her to leave him, but she had two children to think of. But Phyllis had made up her mind there was nothing anyone could say to deter her she was going to England.

The months rolled on and Percy was more distant than before, he had not forgotten her outburst, and had not forgiven her for her insolence. It was Megan's birthday and Phyllis took the children out for the day, they had tea at a lovely British tea room in Delhi run by a charming English lady. They had cream tea with jam on the scones and cucumber sandwiches, Owen didn't eat his sandwich he said it was like eating a slug, "I don't want to know how you know it's like eating a slug Owen," Phyllis said, but she ordered a chicken sandwich for him, then she bought a pretty new dress for Megan with pink roses on the hem line.

"Oh, I love it, Mummy, thank you," Megan said swirling around in the new dress. Phyllis was happy to see her daughter smile she knew roses were her favourite flower, and the child seldom had anything to smile about. She bought the children some warm clothes for the trip to England not mentioning it to the children for fear they would accidentally say something to the wrong person.

Christmas was low key, as usual Phyllis had made a huge fuss of the children on Christmas day, she had bought lots of extravagant gifts for them. She would give them to the children after they had returned from church as she knew Percy would disappear after that, she had no idea where he went and quite frankly, she didn't care, she had made sure that the Christmas table was dressed just as her mother used to do when she was a child, and as Percy never joined them for Christmas dinner, he couldn't ruin their fun. She had instructed the cook to make a typically English roast dinner and she did quite a good job of it even though her Yorkshire puddings were a bit flat, but the beef was delightful. Phyllis gave all the staff a small gift each and some extra money for their families. She gave the children small gifts on the table, a necklace for Megan with diamonds and a topaz set in the middle, and a bangle for Owen with diamonds around it, she had had them inscribed, Megan's said 'To my wonderful daughter, always be strong. Love Mummy', and Owen's said 'To the best son. Love Mummy'. She had also bought them teddies and Owen got a toy train set, and Megan had a china tea set. They had a wonderful time, but Phyllis made sure that they were in bed before their father came home. He didn't bother to see them or wish them a happy Christmas. He didn't visit Phyllis at all and hadn't bought her any gifts. He didn't buy his children gifts either as he thought they had enough toys and were over-indulged by their mother. Phyllis knew he hadn't bought anything for them. Still, she was happy, and she was looking forward to her trip to visit her parents, no gift he bought her would top that. He didn't know what Phyllis liked as he never bothered to find out, she never received gifts from him, and neither did the children. Phyllis had the usual photograph taken as she did every six months, she dressed them up in their finest clothes and visited the studio where she always had their pictures taken, Megan wore a white dress with long white socks and black patent Mary-Jane shoes she held a toy dog not hers just one of the many toys the photographer used to make the children smile, Owen wore a brown velvet pair of shorts and a grey shirt he too had the same shoes and socks as Megan, he chose a toy dog to hold. Little did Phyllis know this was the last photograph she would have done of her precious children.

It was Owen's third birthday on the 17th April, and in just two weeks they will be on a boat sailing to England, Phyllis was so excited she almost forgot to invite his little friends from nursery school to tea at their house. Phyllis and Megan wrapped a gift for pass the parcel. They got the gramophone and records out to play musical statues, it was a lovely afternoon. Phyllis had bought him a small boat to sail on the pond in the park, he loved it. Again, his father didn't bother to acknowledge his birthday. Phyllis was extremely upset, but she knew she would be having a lovely visit with her family in two weeks.

This didn't make Owen feel very happy either as he thought his father didn't love him at all. Megan put her arms around him. "Don't worry Owen, Mummy and I love you very much," she said kissing him on his cheek.

He squirmed away and wiped his cheek smiling, "I love you too Meggy," he said. He soon forgot about being upset and played happily with his friends.

It got closer to the time Percy was due to go on his trip, he wouldn't return until June the 20th. Phyllis spoke to him about the summer, she had been invited to the Rajah's palace again, there would be some old friends going this year also. She had secretly packed two trunks one for the children and one for herself, she put all their warmest clothing in the trunks and the children's winter coats, hats, scarves and gloves. She waited for her husband to go on his trip, and she had made sure her friends would cover for her at the club, but purposefully left a copy of the original schedule so he could see it and think she was committed to things while he was gone. He knew she took the overseas club very seriously. It was planned down to the last detail. She took the trunks to her friend's house saying they were full of old clothes for a fund raiser that she was running for the orphaned children, she often took clothing and other things she didn't want to the overseas club for fund raising, so none of the staff noticed. Most of her friends didn't like Percy so she knew they wouldn't tell him, she took a taxi from her house telling the servants she was visiting a friend who was ill, she knew none of the staff would want to go as they didn't want to get sick too, and cholera was prevalent in the area, they didn't think anything of it. She picked up the trunks from her friend's house, and spoke briefly to her friend she was very nervous but excited too, she got back in to the taxi and told the taxi driver to drive to the port in Bombay where the *Tuscania* was waiting. It was a journey she wouldn't forget in a hurry, at first the sea was calm and the weather was warm as they crossed the Arabian Sea into the Red Sea, and then up the Suez Canal and up the Nile into the Mediterranean Sea. The scenery was magnificent they spent whole days just sitting on deck watching the world go by. She could feel the temperatures drop as they neared the end of the journey and she made sure the children put on their coats when she took them on the deck. They didn't like the cold, neither did Phyllis they had never left the warm climates of India, but Phyllis was so excited at the prospect of seeing her parents, she hardly noticed the rain, as the ship came to a halt at the port of Liverpool. She strained her eyes trying to see if her father was there to pick her and the children up, suddenly she saw him standing by a black car, he had a long coat on and looked very smart with his hat on. He was holding a black umbrella and was very well groomed. As the ship's gang-plank was lowered she couldn't contain herself and the tears flowed down her face as she held her children's hands. "Why are you crying Mummy?" Megan said very concerned.

"I'm so happy Meggy, that's your grandfather over there, he has come to take us to his house."

Owen jumped up and down trying to see, "I can't see Mummy," he said excitedly. Megan looked at the man standing waiting for them he looked very happy to see them.

"I think, Mummy, he has a kind face don't you think?" she said.

Phyllis nodded, "Yes darling he has," she said smiling, as they descended the gang-plank her father greeted them, and he embraced her tightly.

"You silly girl," he whispered, "I was hoping you had changed your mind. You know he will be furious, God knows what he will do." he said as he lifted the children to the back seat of the car. Phyllis sat between them and held them tight, she wasn't worried what Percy could do now they were there she would be seeing her parents and there was nothing he could do about that. She covered their laps in the warm rug her father had put on the back seat so they wouldn't be too cold. The journey through the Liverpool streets was dismal it was still raining, and the rows of houses looked run down and depressing.

"Is it far to your house, Dad?" Phyllis enquired.

"Good God, yes, we live on the other side of London, it will take a good, few hours to get there, it seems I live in this car," he said laughing. "I took your cousin back to Liverpool after his trip, he couldn't wait to return to warmer climates, it has been quite cold here the last few months. I had to wait till the snow cleared before I could take him back, he was going to take the train but the delays would have meant he would have missed the boat back to Singapore. How was your trip, not too bad I hope?" he said.

"Not at all, but we really noticed the change in temperature as soon as we passed the Mediterranean Sea, I thought we would feel sea-sick but we didn't, did we children?"

"Nope," said Owen cheerfully. Megan kept silent.

"What about you Megan did you like the big boat trip?"

"Yes, sir," she answered quietly

"Call me Grandad, sweet child. I am not your father, there is nothing to be afraid of." Phyllis looked very guilty as she hugged her children to her side, her father said nothing for some time. He suddenly said to the children, "Look at the lovely green fields children and no flies," he said laughing. Phyllis relaxed a little, she knew what her father was thinking, and he was right, why on earth did he permit that man to marry his precious daughter, it was obvious he didn't love her. And his daughter was terrified of everyone.

As the countryside passed by, the children fell asleep. Phyllis's father spoke very quietly, as not to wake them, "I'm so happy to see you, darling," he said in earnest, "Mum has got lots of lovely food ready for you and the children when we arrive, I'm really rather hungry aren't you?"

"I am getting that way yes, Dad," she said.

"Do you think Percy will be very angry with you?" he asked.

"Furious, now that I think of it, I'm a little worried that he will make sure I never do this again," she said, "I hate it there without you Dad, I miss Mum and the rest of the family. I have missed all the weddings and new babies and everything. I have no one to talk to, no one who cares about my children or me, I'm left with the servants for company, and only one can speak English," she said feeling miserable.

"I'm sorry darling, I know the timing could have been better, but if I had waited any longer the job opening would have gone to someone else," he said, "India is changing we had to leave, I should have said no to this marriage, he was much too old to be the kind of husband I would have wanted for you, but Mum insisted he was a good match. I think she wanted you to be well off, she knew you like the finer things, but I'm sure when she finds out how he is towards you and the children, she will be sorry she ever heard of Percy at all," he said.

Phyllis sat quietly for a few moments thinking, she wished she hadn't married Percy, she could have moved to England with her family and met a nicer man altogether.

"What are you thinking about darling?" her father asked looking at her in the mirror.

"Oh, nothing, Dad," she said, "I was hoping I get a good visit in before Percy comes and orders me home," she said.

"I hope that's all he does," her father said, "he sounds like a cad, but divorce is not the answer, he will make sure you don't take the children with you and they will have a terrible life with him, you must stay for their sakes," he said.

Phyllis knew he was right, she sighed. "He is a powerful man, and no one would go up against him," she said. She had seen first-hand what he could be like and wasn't averse to hitting her, but she would never tell her father, that would just add to his worries. She would have a nice visit and go back to India and take whatever punishment he dealt her.

"Are we there yet?" came a small groggy voice beside her.

"No darling it's a little further," Phyllis said looking at her father hopefully.

Her father said, "It's another hour at least depending on the traffic," he said smiling at the little boy in the back seat with his hair sticking up as he had been leaning on his mother's lap, Phyllis smoothed it down.

Suddenly Meg sat upright looking very scared, "He's coming," she said, "he's coming, and he's very angry," she said in a panic.

"Who's coming darling?" Phyllis said putting her arm around Meg to calm her.

"Father, he knows we have gone. He is getting on a boat he's very angry."

"Don't be silly darling, he isn't due back home for weeks, he couldn't know," Phyllis said trying to reassure Megan.

"Yes, he does, someone told him. He's coming to take us away, Mummy, please don't let him take us!" she cried.

"It's all right darling, he won't take you away, it was just a dream, a silly dream that's all." But Phyllis knew Meg could be right, she had had dreams before that came true, she held her daughter for the next hour, rocking her gently.

They arrived at her parent's house in Norfolk Avenue. It had stopped raining as her father parked the car in front of the detached house. It was on the corner of the street and had a large hedge around the front and side of the front garden, there was a slight incline towards the garage in front of the house and her mother was standing in the doorway smiling excitedly. As Phyllis got out of the car, her younger brother Henry came out of the house to help her father with the bags.

"Hi, sis." he said smiling broadly.

"You've grown!" she said smiling back, but her father wasn't smiling.

"Henry! why aren't you at school," Henry stopped in front of his father.

"Well, I had a slight disagreement with one of my teachers', Dad, and was sent home," he said nervously.

"EXPELLED!" his father shouted.

"No, Dad, just suspended for a week," he said.

His mother chimed in, "And he has detention when he gets back too, I don't know Henry you won't get anywhere by arguing with your teachers," she said.

"Honestly, Mum, I just pointed out she was grammatically incorrect, and she started to scream at me."

"Was she wrong?" his father asked.

"Yes, she was wrong, but it didn't help that I screamed back at her," Henry said laughing. "Okay, sis. I'll take this up to the spare room for you." He turned to his mother. "When is dinner, Mum? I'm starving."

She smiled at him. "You and your stomach," she said playfully, he laughed as he entered the house and dived up the stairs as though Phyllis's trunks were light as a feather.

Phyllis smiled at her mother. "Hello, Mum," she said embracing her.

"Hello, darling, how was the boat — didn't get seasick, did you?" she said looking at the children holding on to the back of their mother's skirt. "Come along let's get inside in the warm," she said. As they all entered the house, they felt the warmth of

27

the fire in the lounge, there was a small boy playing with some soldiers sitting in front of the fire.

"Don't sit so close to the fire, Richard," their father said shunting the child towards the couch.

"Oh, Dad I'm cold," he complained.

"Well put another jumper on," his mother scolded. "I told you this morning you wouldn't be warm enough in that shirt."

The boy looked at Meg and Owen and scowled. Meg stepped back but Owen said, "Cor, can I play with those?" Pointing at the soldiers.

"No, they are mine," Richard snapped.

"Oh dear," Phyllis said sitting on the couch beside Richard. "That's not very nice is it, Richard? We are your family you should be kinder."

"Yes, and guests in our home," their mother snapped. "You should share your toys or you will have to go to your room," she said stiffly.

"I'm your big sister," Phyllis said, "and these are your niece and nephew. This is Megan and this is Owen, we have come all the way from India to see you." As Henry came bounding into the room, he ruffled Owen's hair and picked him up playfully. Phyllis took a deep breath and said, "Henry, he's not used to people picking him up," but Owen was laughing as Henry put him on his shoulders. Megan smiled, she had never heard her brother giggle like that.

"Come on, kids, I'll take you to see the rest of the house if Richard is being selfish with his toys, I'll find you some better ones to play with." Megan finally let go of her mother's skirt and happily went with her uncle, he was a jolly fellow, and suddenly Megan wasn't scared.

Phyllis looked worried. "Be gentle with them, won't you,

Henry."

He looked back at Phyllis as he left the room with the two children in tow. "Don't worry so much sis, they are fine with me, aren't you, children?"

Owen giggled, "Yes, we are fine, Mummy." Megan smiled at her mother as she left the room with Henry.

"So," her mother said giving her daughter a cup of tea. "How did you get Percy to agree to let you come, I thought he said you couldn't come."

Phyllis looked confused. "Didn't Dad tell you, I was sick of waiting, so I left without him knowing."

Her mother's face was a mixture of shock and horror. "You mean he doesn't know?" Her mother said. "Oh Phyllis, what have you done," she said, sitting down on the couch. "He isn't used to people defying him, god knows what he will do when he finds out."

"I had to come, Mum, I was suffocating there, everyone has left India I only have a few friends left. Next-to-no family, even cousin Cicely is moving to England soon, the rest of the cousins have either gone to Canada or America, I'm almost totally alone, Mum," she started to cry. "Why did I have to marry someone like Percy?" she said.

Her mother passed a handkerchief to her and as she blew her nose her father came and sat next to her and put his arm around her shoulder. "Chin up, old love," he said softly.

"I'm trying to be strong, but when everyone you know is moving away, and I'm stuck in India. I can't see Percy ever moving here. Or anywhere, can you?" she said questioningly.

"I don't know darling," her mother said. "India is not the same any more there is too much unrest. I was talking to my brother Gottfried before he died, he thought the British would have to leave India before long, he gave it another ten years, maybe less, it doesn't make sense to stay where you are not wanted," she said.

"I'm sorry, Mum, to hear about Uncle Gottfried, I know how close you were."

"Thank you, dear, it was very unexpected," she said, "but back to what I was saying — he thought the unrest would escalate, the natives really don't want the British there any longer."

"Exactly," Phyllis said suddenly. "I'm not wanted. Percy doesn't love me, and he certainly doesn't love our children, he just sees us as possessions. He's never home and when he is, he's off with those stupid masons."

"Yes, but darling he gives you a very good life, you never have to worry about money, you have a lovely house and servants," her mother interjected.

"What's the point of having those things, Mum when you don't have love," Phyllis said through her tears. "He doesn't even love his children, you should see how he treats them, they are petrified of him, he makes Owen eat hot food and he knows he hates it. Megan shakes uncontrollably when he's around, he has never said a kind word to her in her life, all because she is a girl. I've never heard of anything so cold in my life," she said. "Dad wasn't like that with us, and he has five daughters," she said blowing her nose again.

Her father laughed. "What would be the point, you would all beat me," he said as he hugged her.

"I'm serious, Dad, have you ever heard anything so cold as to not love your child, even when I gave him a son, he wasn't much nicer," she said.

"You can't leave him, Phyllis, think of the children he won't let you have them," her mother said, almost crying herself. "I wish I had known he was this way before I introduced him to you. I just thought he could give you everything you would want."

"Oh, he does," Phyllis said. "But he doesn't know how to love, even when he visits my bed, he isn't gentle, he just takes what he wants and leaves, he never kisses me or hugs me, I don't remember when he last smiled at me let alone anything else, is he really happy with me? Or am I just a status symbol, oh, look at my young wife, isn't she pretty."

"Well, let's eat, the food is getting cold," her father said trying to change the subject. "We can decide what to do after the children have gone to bed." They all agreed.

Her mother called everyone to the table, Megan sat as close to her uncle Henry as she could and Owen sat the other side of him trying to look bigger, he puffed out his chest looking very much older than three. His mother put all sorts of different things on his plate, saying, "Eat what you can, darling, all right."

"Mum, can you help Megan with the meat, she hasn't quite got the action of cutting it up yet. Still, she's very clever aren't you darling?"

Megan sat smiling at her mother, "Yes, Mummy," she said sweetly.

Richard sat scowling at the new additions to his family, stuffing food into his mouth and chewing loudly, his mother looked at him. "Richard, must you eat like a guttersnipe," she said sighing.

"Where is everyone else? Do they know I'm here?" Phyllis said as they ate.

"Errol is still in Scotland," her father said, "he is planning a visit next year — what with the boys and the new house they are a trifle busy at present, he does send his love and wishes he could be here to see you," he said.

"Kitty will be over later with the children. You can help me make some cakes and sandwiches for tea," her mother said, as she gave Richard more food. "Freda and Jean will be home from work at five-thirty. I think Freda's beau is coming this evening he is in the air force, a very nice young man, Tom's his name," she said. "Unfortunately, Pauline is still at school," her mother said.

"So should Henry be!" her father interjected,

"She won't be home until May bank holiday," her mother continued, looking at her husband slightly annoyed at the interruption. "She had just been home last week, you just missed her. However, I'm sure she would love to see you on 6th May, if you are still here," she said, "and really, Cyril, Henry was right to challenge his teacher," she said, smiling at her wayward son. "If she doesn't know simple grammar. She is an English teacher after all," she said. "I'm a little concerned at the choice of schools we sent him to," she said, taking a sip of water.

"I agree," her husband said, "but he knows not to be rude to people, doesn't he?"

"Of course, it was a little rude to shout back at her, but had she been correct in her teaching this wouldn't have been at all necessary."

"So, you agree with me, but I'm wrong," he said quizzically.

"Yes," she said laughing, they all laughed. Henry and Errol had attended La Martinier College for Boys in Lucknow, Cyril thought if it wasn't for the Howe family all attending, they would have half the students. Unfortunately, his youngest son wouldn't be attending.

After lunch, the children went off to explore the garden with Henry, Richard towing behind them. He wasn't sure he liked these new kids, they were way too quiet for his liking, and that little one looked too lovingly at his soldiers, but Richard had stashed them away so he couldn't touch them.

Megan was in awe of the greenhouse full of beautiful flowers, her grandmother's pride and joy. while Henry was preoccupied with Owen, Richard whispered into Megan's ear, "I like the big red ones," he said "I like to take the heads off and make a path with the petals," he said, as Megan's eyes grew bigger at the prospect of picking the beautiful blooms. Richard left her alone with her thoughts and caught Henry up, who was telling Owen that the grass was a bit wet to walk on right now so he should stay on the patio.

As he turned around, he noticed Megan dancing inside the greenhouse he laughed. "What are you doing, sweet girl?" he said as he walked closer. He stopped and gasped, "Megan, what are you doing?" he shouted. Megan stopped dancing, she had picked one of the beautiful blooms and was singing he loves me, he loves me not, while picking off the petals and throwing them onto the floor of the greenhouse. Henry took the flower from her, "You should never touch mother's flowers, that was a very naughty thing to do!" he said crossly.

"But Richard said I could," she protested tearfully.
Henry looked at Richard accusingly Richard shrugged his shoulders, "No I didn't!" he said.

Henry took the children back into the house and told his mother what had happened. Of course, by this time Megan was crying uncontrollably as her mother was trying to console her, her grandmother had rushed out to see the damage to her prized blooms, when she returned she was quite calm.

"It's all right," she said, "there are enough left for the show on Saturday. Megan had only picked one thank goodness."

Phyllis sighed with relief.

"I'm so sorry, Grandmother," Megan said tearfully, "I didn't know they were so special and Richard told me he was allowed to pick them."

Winifred looked at Richard, "Why on earth would you say that, Richard, you know they are my special ones for the show on Saturday. Did you want to get Megan into trouble?" she said as she was trying to keep her temper.

"I didn't say anything of the sort," he said stiffly. "She misunderstood me."

"I didn't," Megan shouted, "you said you like to pick off the heads and make a path with them!"

"Well luckily she didn't pick them all," Henry said, "really Richard you are such a brat sometimes, come on kids let's go to my room and find some toys to play with. Owen do you like chess?" he said loudly, he knew Richard loved to play chess with his brother, Richard looked very angry.

Their father had been out to get an evening paper, and he came back just in time to see Winifred sending Richard to his room, "What has he done now?" he exclaimed.

"I'll tell you later dear, I have to get tea sorted out," as she hurriedly went to the kitchen.

Phyllis was just putting the last dishes into the cabinet, she was upset. "I'm sorry about your flowers, Mum, she does love them so," she said.

"It wasn't her fault, Richard encouraged her to pick them, she wasn't to know," her mother said. "I don't know why he is such a naughty boy, all you children were very well behaved when you were young, Pauline is a good girl, but Richard is moody and selfish. I don't know where he gets it from, no one has been that way to him, Henry and Pauline treat him very well, always happy to entertain him. Still, he never shares his toys with the other children, Robert and Kathy have taken to bringing their toys with them when they visit us. I'm sure everyone thinks we overindulge him. I don't think I have one nice photograph of him, he's always grumpy," she said wiping the sides down getting ready to bake some scones.

"I'm sure he will grow out of it, Mum," Phyllis said trying to make her mother feel better.

"Maybe I was too old to have another child," Winifred said, "your children are very well behaved."

Phyllis looked at her mother. "They are scared to death of everything, a bully governs their lives," she said bitterly. "I dread to think what he will do when I return to India, and I have a mind not to go back at all," she said.

Her mother took a deep breath. "Oh, don't be foolish, Phyllis, do you know what he could do if you didn't, he could divorce you, leave you without a penny, and take your children from you."

"Could he take the children, Dad?" she said turning to her father who was sitting reading his paper at the kitchen table.

"Yes, he could, he is the breadwinner, he could take the children easily," her father said, trying not to scare his daughter, as he sipped a cup of tea. He was reading the weather, "Good lord," he said, "they say it's going to snow the worst snowstorm in sixty years, would you believe it? We had better make sure we get more coal for the fires dear," it was clear he didn't want to discuss his daughter's husband any longer.

"Come on, Cyril, I need the table, could you possibly go to the lounge," Winifred said trying to shoo him out of the kitchen.

He got up from the table taking his tea and his newspaper and left the room, muttering something about lights in the middle of the roads, saying "would you believe it, that's a lot of lights, the whole country!"

Phyllis sat there in shock, "What have I done?" she cried.

"Don't worry about it now, dear," her mother said trying to comfort Phyllis, "he might not do anything, we are worrying before we know what he will do."

"I hope you are right, Mum," Phyllis said. She got up to butter the bread for the sandwiches for tea, her mother sliced the cucumber and checked the scones weren't burning. Phyllis started making the Victoria sandwich as she knew Kitty loved her cakes, she was excited to see her sister as she hadn't seen them since before her marriage six years ago, and she hadn't met her youngest son Patrick yet either, he was about Owen's age. She had forgotten what the other two even looked like, Robert and Kathy were babies when she had last seen them. By the time they had finished making the sandwiches, cakes and scones everyone was assembling in the dining room.

Kitty had arrived with her husband, Mervyn, and the children were playing in the living room and getting to know their cousins. Henry and Mervyn went into the garden to have a smoke. Phyllis's mother had to delegate. "Oh, Kitty darling, could you put the sandwiches on the table for me, there's a love, and Phyllis that Victoria sandwich looks lovely, could you slice it, it'll have to be thinly as, oh my gosh, there are so many children, no Patrick don't pull at the table-cloth dear," she said.

Kitty put the sandwiches down and tackled her youngest onto a chair, the other two children were sitting nicely as was Megan and Owen by this time, but Richard was still in his room.

Phyllis managed to get fourteen slices out of her cake, not too small either, she looked at her handiwork and smiled licking jam from her fingers. There were more than twenty scones and piles of sandwiches, with chicken, spam and cucumber, luckily her mother had four teapots. As everyone sat down Jean and Freda came home. "Oh, just in time," they said, sitting at the huge dining table.

Their mother had just called Richard to the table, he wasn't happy. "What's wrong with you, grumpy face?" Jean said making a face at him. He didn't think that was funny and sat with his arms crossed until he realised, he couldn't eat like that. His mother put a sandwich on his plate, and he ate it so noisily that all the children looked at him in amazement.

"Gosh!" Robert said, "if I ate like that my mother would put me out in the garden," he said looking at Richard wide-eyed.

Kitty looked at her son, "Robert, I wouldn't put you in the garden."

"But Mummy, that's what you said yesterday when I made a noise eating my soup."

"Darling, you were slurping, one doesn't slurp," she said sticking her nose in the air.

Phyllis laughed. "Do you remember that nanny we had, she used to say that didn't she? What a funny woman she was, what was her name mother?"

"Grace," her mother said. "I inherited her from my cousin,

she came with stella credentials. She had been a nanny to the Battenburges until she resigned, ghastly turn of events, I don't quite know what happened but they didn't like her very much I don't think."

"I don't blame them," Kitty said, "she was a strange creature."

"Yes, but she taught us to eat properly," Phyllis said.

"And she was getting along in years," their mother said in her defence.

"Yes, unfortunately some of you didn't pass the knowledge on to your children," their father said, looking at Robert over his glasses.

"Oh, Dad, he's young still," Kitty said defending her son.

"You were younger than he is," their mother said. They all turned to her looking intently, then at Richard accusingly. "Oh, all right, I think we are all guilty of neglecting to teach our children table manners," she said going very red. "All you older ones ate impeccably."

"So what happened to Richard? Really Mother you are too soft on him," Kitty said looking at her mother.

"Well, I think it's because I had a nanny for you older children, it was so much easier back then in India, but nannies are very expensive in England, and we couldn't possibly warrant the expenditure. It's not like we have the social life we used to have back in the old days, England is so different to what we had been used to, garden parties and balls, we are lucky to attend the Christmas do here," she said laughing.

Megan and Owen sat listening to the family talking over tea, they looked at each other and shrugged their shoulders and carried on eating the delicious food. They had never seen anyone talk so much at the dinner table, they were never allowed to speak to their father that way or their mother, it took quite a while to get used to it.

When their mother was tucking them in that night, they both asked if her father would beat her and her sister, as they spoke a little rudely in front of him today.

"No, why do you ask?" Phyllis said quite shocked that they would think her father capable of such a thing.

"Well, if we spoke like that in front of our father, he most definitely would beat us," Megan said.

"Yes, well, your father isn't very kind, is he?" she said trying not to speak too ill of their father as they still had to live with him when they returned to India, a thought she didn't want to have, so soon after just arriving. "Go to sleep now my darlings," she said as she tucked them in one last time and kissed their heads softly, and left the room. "Shall I leave the door open a little or are you all right with it shut?" she said as she went through the door.

"We are all right with it closed, Mother I'll take care of Owen," Megan said, hugging Owen close to her, he closed his eyes,

"Good night then, children, see you in the morning."

"Good night, mother," they chimed.

Phyllis went downstairs, Kitty was sitting on the footstool in front of her father, she looked like she had been crying.

"Oh Lord, what's the matter?" Phyllis said looking at everyone else.

Her mother entered the room, she had just put Richard to bed. "What's wrong with you?" she said looking around the room.

"I don't know," Phyllis said. "They were like this when I came in, just now."

Kitty got up and hugged her sister, "I'm so glad to see you Phil, but I'm worried you did something foolish by coming here against your husband's wishes. What do you think he will do?" she asked.

"I know," Phyllis said quietly looking at the floor, "I wasn't thinking. I just wanted to see my family, for the last five years I've been asking him and he said next year, next year. I just snapped. He has never minded me going to the mountains for months without him without so much as a postcard to us. I sent him several postcards he never answered, so why would this be any different," she said.

"Well, I for one, don't think he will do anything," Henry said. "It's no different to going to the mountains, is it? And that happens every year."

"Yes, but he isn't a reasonable man," Cyril said.

Henry turned to Phyllis. "He will just make you aware he isn't happy, won't he?" he said.

"That's if he cares," Phyllis said sulkily.

"Is that why you disobeyed him?" Winifred said.

"No, I told you I just wanted to visit you, I haven't seen any of you in almost five years," Phyllis said. "All my relatives in India are moving away or have died, I have but a handful of friends left, I should be happily married, but I'm not!" she said, almost crying. "All of you are happy, aren't you?" she said looking at Kitty. "Your husband loves you, does he not, Kitty?"

"Yes, of course he does," Kitty said.

"And your children?" Phyllis asked,

"Yes of course," Kitty said again.

"Well, mine doesn't, he hates my daughter, the love of my life, she brings me such joy, and he hates her, and then I produce a son and heir, but still he isn't kind to him, he's a cruel man and doesn't love them and he doesn't love me," she said tearfully, "and you are all happy. Is it so bad to want to be happy too?" she said.

"I think you are over exaggerating, Phyllis, no one is that bad!" Henry said. His parents both looked at the young man, his father shaking his head, his mother put her hands on his shoulders.

"Yes, I think he is that bad, Henry," she said with a sigh, "Phyllis has never lied to us in all her life," she said.

"I believe every word," Cyril said, sighing.

"Why on earth did you marry such a cad then?" Henry shouted. "Those poor kids they are so sweet and innocent, well if he comes here, I'll show him a thing or two!" he said forcefully.

"I don't see what we could possibly do if he does come here, you are married," Cyril said, "and they are his children, the breadwinner has the ultimate say even if she divorces him, he will get custody of the children." Cyril sighed. "I'm tired my dears, I'm going to bed," he said, kissing the tops of each of his children's heads and his wife as he retired to bed.

They all looked at each other, Winifred said, "I'm going to make a cup of cocoa does anyone want one?" she asked.

"No thanks, Mum, I need something a little stronger. Henry could you possibly?" Kitty said waving her empty whisky glass at him.

"Yes, of course. Phil, do you want one?" Henry said.

"Yes, please, Henry," she said, taking a seat by the fire.

41

Jean and Freda went with their mother to make cocoa.

"Is Tom coming tonight Freda?" her mother asked.

"Not tonight, Mum, I asked him not to as it was Phil's first night and I thought everyone would be gossiping and he would get left out, I didn't want him to feel awkward."

Her mother smiled at her saying, "Very wise under the circumstances, you are so thoughtful Freda."

Jean lit up a cigarette and went outside in the garden. Freda followed her and they sat on the garden bench smoking and drinking their cocoa.

Kitty, Henry and Phyllis were sat silently when Winifred returned with her cocoa, she sat next to Phyllis and put her hand on her knee. "It will work out, darling, I'm sure," she said. Henry passed Phyllis a large whisky glass half full of whisky, Winifred looked at her son. "Is that Dad's whisky?" she asked.

"Yes, he did say we could have it," Henry said pouring himself a glass, his mother nodded.

Phyllis was almost in tears. "I'm sorry, Mum, I should have stayed at home, now I've dragged you and Dad into it. I can see Dad isn't happy about it."

Her mother took a sip of her cocoa and said, "Dad loves you, Phyllis, he always has, he's just afraid he can't protect you from this," her mother said. "It's all my stupid fault, I thought he would take care of you, like your father has taken care of me, I knew you like the same things as I do, I just wanted you to have a lovely life, but you don't, and now I feel responsible," she said.

"Oh no, Mum don't," Phyllis said, holding her mother's hand, "you were only trying to make sure I had a good life, how were you to know?" Phyllis said, looking at her tearful mother.

"Anyway, now I know why he wasn't married before," her mother said, bitterly.

"I just hope nothing happens," Kitty said. "If he comes here and takes the children, I don't think I could watch, and what would he do with them when he got them," she said, taking a huge swig of her whisky.

"They are frightened of him," Phyllis said. "They have always been frightened of him. He isn't a loving father like Dad, I don't know why I didn't see this before I married him," she said. "He seemed so nice back then, but as soon as we were married, he changed, he was cold and distant."

"It was lovely of Mervyn to take the children home and put them to bed so you could visit a while, Kitty," Winifred said, trying to change the subject.

"Yes, he's a darling like that," Kitty said. "We had agreed that he would do that before we arrived, he knew I wanted to see Phil and catch up."

Phyllis smiled at her sister, "I really am glad your husband is a darling, Kitty," she said smiling.

"He was always a thoughtful child," Winifred said. "I remember when he was small, we used to have holidays with Lilly and Robert."

"Yes, I remember," Phyllis said, wistfully.

"I bet the weather was quite a shock," Kitty said, laughing.

"Yes," Phyllis said. "I have never felt so cold, the children didn't like it either, it was quite a shock."

"Am I taking you home later or am I sleeping on the couch?" Henry asked Kitty.

"You are a darling, Henry, you can have your bed we will probably be up most of the night talking," Kitty said, looking at her sister. "I've missed you so terribly," she said. "Life just isn't the same as it was. Errol isn't here and you are not either. I miss you both so terribly," she said.

"Yes, I have missed you all, it's so different without knowing you are just a car journey away, letters take so long to arrive and there isn't enough paper in the world to say everything, and some things you just can't write in a letter, you know, secrets and the like, girly things," Phyllis said.

"Wait…" said Henry. "I just need to vomit," he said, making fun of the two sisters, then he got out his pipe and filled it with tobacco.

"Oh no, my little baby brother, smoking," Phyllis said, shocked that he had grown up so fast. "Drinking Dad's whisky and smoking, I can't take it," she said. "Just yesterday you were sitting on my knee singing nursery rhymes."

Henry smiled at his sister. "I loved those days," he said, ruefully.

Winifred yawned. "I think I'm off to bed now darlings, see you in the morning, and Henry don't drink too much you will dear, you will have to take Kitty home tomorrow."

"No, that's all right, Mum, Mervyn is coming to get me," Kitty said.

"Well, don't drink all of Dad's whisky," she said, as she was heading for the door.

Henry looked at his father's bottle, it was almost empty. "Okay, Mum," he said, looking wide-eyed at his sisters, when their mother had gone, he showed them the bottle.

"That's all right, I'll go and get some more for him tomorrow," Phyllis said. "That's the least I can do after the mess I've caused."

They spent the next few hours talking about married life and Kitty's wedding that Phyllis had missed, they spoke about their older brother Errol and his wife Jessie. Phyllis had missed their wedding also, Phyllis had met Jessie but didn't know her well, Kitty spoke kindly of them, Errol always had a smile on his face and they were always happy.

"You should see their boys, they are the sweetest children you could ever meet, Mervyn and I went up when William was born, they are such darlings," Kitty said.

They were planning a trip next summer, as Errol was working hard, they had moved from Canada and are living in Scotland. "I think they have built their new house in Glasgow, Mum and Dad had gone to visit them in Canada in 1932 but were so happy when Errol had found a commission in Scotland. they lived with Jessie's parents until their house was ready. Her parents were good people, Mum and Dad get along very well with the Inglis's."

Phyllis always wondered what Percy's parents were like as she had never met them. They were not at their wedding, and he never spoke about them, she took it they had passed away before they had met. They never had visitors at the house in all the five years they had lived there. He always went out to see his friends, they never came to visit them.

Time flew by, and Phyllis found herself yawning. "I really must go to bed," she said. "I'll never get up for the children in the morning." Kitty was falling asleep on the couch, but Henry being the gentleman he was, told her to go his room and sleep, he would take the couch, Kitty tried to argue, but Henry was having none of it. He ordered his older sister to bed she shrugged her shoulders and followed Phyllis upstairs.

The next day it was raining again, Phyllis woke to the sounds of children giggling, it made her smile, she seldom heard giggling from her children, she got up to see what they were giggling about. As she entered the lounge, she saw her brother Henry still fast asleep on the couch, and her little brother Richard tickling Henry's nose with a feather from his mother's hat, Megan and Owen were hiding behind the door watching Richard and Henry, the feather made Henry's nose twitch as he batted it away the children thought it was so funny. Richard changed the direction the feather came from, suddenly Henry jumped up and grabbed his little brother and tickled him, at first Megan hid further behind the door, then she followed Owen out laughing at the melee, it was the first time Phyllis had seen Richard smile since they got there and she felt a little relieved as the ice was definitely broken between the children. Megan had forgiven Richard for trying to get her into trouble the day before and Richard had even allowed Owen to play with his soldiers. The children played happily all morning, and in the afternoon, Henry had set up two chess sets so all the children could play — Henry showed Owen how to play and Richard showed Megan, as soon as Owen seemed to get the hang of it they swapped, Megan played Henry and Owen played Richard. Winifred was relieved too, Richard never had anyone to play with his own age, he seemed to warm to the children and even allowed Owen to win at chess, but for three years old he was very good at the game, then they got the ludo out and they all played. Henry was so good with children, he always played fair, he told Richard a gentleman always let ladies have best of everything, and if he wanted to grow up a fine gentleman he needed to practise on Megan. At dinner he pulled her chair out for her and gave her a serviette for her lap, he ate nicely too which pleased his mother. His father smiled at Henry, "Good job son," he said. Henry said he didn't know what he was talking about Richard had always been a gentleman.

Before they knew it, it was time for bed. As Phyllis was

tucking her children in Megan said, "Do you think Grandmother and Grandfather would let us stay here, Mummy," she said, sleepily.

"I'm afraid not, darling," she said. "We have to return to India, or father may be even more angry."

"You mean angrier than he is already?" Megan said.

"What do you mean, darling?" Phyllis said.

"Well, I think he is angry with me, your father and brothers are not like that, Grandfather treats you all like you treat Owen and I. Maybe father is angry all the time he doesn't seem to like me at all," she said.

"Well, I love you with all my heart Megan and don't you ever forget that whatever happens in the future you must never forget how much I love you both," Phyllis said, with a tear in her eye. "Oh," she said. "I have dust in my eye, I'll be back in a moment I have to go to bathroom," she said. She rushed to the bathroom and grabbed a towel from the rail and stuffed it over her face and cried into it muffling the sound, she returned when she felt she could control herself, she could never let Megan see how frightened she was of losing her precious children, she tucked the children in and read a story, kissed them goodnight and went downstairs to the lounge.

Winifred saw that Phyllis had been crying. "What's the matter, dear?" she said.

"Oh, Mum, I love my children so much. They don't want to go back to India, they want to stay here with you, but I have to go home or Percy will be horrendous," she said, trying not to cry again.

Her mother hugged her tight saying, "Listen, Dad was saying he is going to see the Jubilee procession next week why don't you go with him then he can take you to the boat the day after on the 7th May. He can see the whole thing from the windows in his office in Whitehall," she said.

"Oh, that sounds lovely, Mum," Phyllis said.

"I'll look after the children," her mother said. "Henry and I will take them to the park. Pauline will be home too."

"Really, Mum?" Phyllis said. "I haven't seen the Palace or the Trouping of the Colour, I would love that," she said, with a happy smile.

The week flew by as it always does when you are having so much fun, tea's at their Aunt Kitty's house playing with their cousins. Megan liked Kathy as she was so much bigger than Megan, and very kind, they played with Kathy's dolls and had their own little tea party, she had even given Megan a doll to play with.

"You can give it back when you go home," she said, cheerily.

"Oh, thank you," Megan said, holding the doll carefully. "I promise I'll take good care of it, Kathy."

Owen had fun too as Patrick was a few months younger than he was. it was nice not being the youngest person in the room, and Robert was a very kind chap and he allowed them all to play in his fort that his father had built him in the garden.

"I liked playing with Robert and Patrick today, Mother," Owen said, as they took a taxi home.

"I loved it too," Megan said. "Look what Kathy has let me borrow until we go home," she said, showing off the doll.

"Yes, they are all very lovely," Phyllis said, hugging her children close.

6th May 1935, Phyllis got up early she was excited to go to the procession, it wasn't raining for a change, the sun was shining.

"What a lovely day," she said to her mother, who was

buttering some bread for the children's breakfast. She had made boiled eggs and soldiers which was Richard's favourite, Megan and Owen seemed to be enjoying them too, as she made a pot of tea, Phyllis put out cups for her mother and father and herself.

"No Henry this morning?" she enquired.

"He was up late last night, studying," Winifred said. "He has his exams soon," she added. They drank their tea and Phyllis made some toast, she was far too excited to eat anything else, her mother had packed them both some sandwiches and a flask of tea, she had wrapped a few scones in a serviette and put it all in a bag for them to take with them. She had packed a lovely picnic for the children and Henry and herself to take to the park, and the children were excitedly talking about taking a ball with them.

It was time for Phyllis to leave she had put her best day time dress on, navy blue with small white flowers, and a lace collar with a thin belt around the middle, she kissed her children and hoped they had a wonderful day. She expected Megan to fret, but she didn't, she said to her mother, "Have the best day ever Mummy, we are going to have fun with Grandmother and Uncle Henry in the park, I hope you don't miss us too much," she said, with a worried look.

"I will try to have fun even though you won't be with me, I'll keep you in my heart," she said, kissing her daughter tenderly on her forehead. As she left the house the children waved from the window as her father drove away. It wasn't far to her father's offices in Whitehall, some of his colleagues were already there and had placed some chairs at the windows. Phyllis excitedly sat looking out, as the sun shone down the street below there were quite a few people standing on each side of the pavement, her father passed her a sandwich she placed it on her lap but didn't open it as she was far too excited to eat. She noticed a picture of

Sir John Simon on the wall and asked her father who he was.

"That's my boss," he explained. "The Secretary of State and Foreign Affairs, but he was running for the position of Chancellor of the Exchequer."

"Oh," she said. "Will he be coming here today?"

"Not today, he has other duties to attend to," he said. As they were talking the sounds from outside got louder and the people in the street started to cheer, Phyllis looked out of the window.

Sure enough, she saw the carriages carrying the King himself and his wife Queen Mary, closely behind was another carriage carrying the Prince of Wales.

Phyllis was in awe she had never seen a British monarch, she had seen plenty of Maharajas and Indian princes and princesses, but never had she seen the pomp and pageantry of the British court.

The day was coming to an end, and it was time to go home, as her father drove to Surrey, Phyllis chattered away happily, reliving every moment.

"I'm glad you enjoyed it, Phil," her father said in earnest.

"Yes, I loved every moment of it, Dad, it was fabulous, I can't wait to tell mother and the children all about it."

Winifred had prepared the dinner, as usual, and the family sat in the dining room as Phyllis was relaying the day.

"What did the king look like, Phil?" Henry said, listening intently.

"He looked very grand for an old gentleman, and the queen was all in whites and cream furs she looked every bit like you would expect a queen to look like, she had a lovely kind smile, she looked right at me and waved," she said excitedly.

"It was nice to see the king fit and well," Cyril said. "He was very ill not three months ago, they feared the worst, but she nursed him back to health refusing to let him die."

The children listened in awe. After dinner the children played kings and queen, wearing her grandmother's fur stole, Megan pranced around the lounge waving at the adults just like a queen. The kings, Richard and Owen, bowing low to Megan and giving her a seat on the footstool she pretended she was giving a speech. Just then Cyril told the children to hush as the real king's speech was on the radio. They sat listening, as the king spoke about the love of his people and how proud he was of them. He spoke of the hope for the general public a job for everyone, he looked to the future for hope and his sons to become useful citizens, and to all the children he asked them to remember that they would be the citizens of the future, to give their all for their country, no words could express his deep feeling for his people and may God bless them.

They sat in silence for a while, then Owen said out loud, "Grandmother has made fudge, it tastes wonderful." They all laughed at him and Winifred dished out some to the children.

"Mummy, you should try this, it tastes like heaven," he said. Phyllis helped herself to a piece she didn't usually eat sweets but she never could turn down a piece of her mother's fudge. It was time for bed, the realisation that they would be going home tomorrow hit hard, Phyllis hadn't told the children so she had to pack their things when they had gone to bed. After kissing them goodnight she started to pack, there was a knock at the door, it was a policeman asking for Phyllis, she went to the door, the policeman said that tomorrow her husband would be coming to take the children home. Phyllis told him that she herself was going home tomorrow, and there was no need for him to come and take them. Suddenly the car door opened and there stood Percy. "How dare you disobey me! I didn't give you permission to take my children overseas," he said.

Phyllis started to apologise, but he said, "Spare me your excuses I will be picking the children up in the morning at nine a.m. have them ready, you may stay here as long as you like but if you want to see your children again, I suggest you go back to India."

Cyril decided he had heard enough. "What do you mean, if she wants to see the children again?" he said. "She is their mother, and she has every right to see them."

"I have decided to send them to boarding school in Belgium. A convent school, they will go there until I deem to move them," he said airily.

"No!" Phyllis shouted. "You can't, they need me. I'm sorry Percy, I will never disobey you again I promise, but please don't punish them they have done nothing."

"You are right, Phyllis, you will never do it again, or you won't see them ever again," he said.

Cyril stood his ground. "Where is it you are taking the children, Percival!" he said trying to control his temper.

"The convent school is in Bruges, it has a very good academic record, I had decided they would attend the school next year, but they have room for them now so I will be taking them there tomorrow. I will be here at nine a.m. sharp. Don't keep me waiting, or I will be forced to bring a policeman with me," he said.

Phyllis collapsed, her mother caught her before she hit the floor, Cyril turned to help his daughter and as he turned back, Percy had driven off,

"Coward! Cad!" he shouted after him.

"Oh, Cyril what are we to do?" Winifred said, trying to bring Phyllis around. "Henry, get the smelling salts, would you?" she said, gently tapping her daughters face. Phyllis came to, she sat up

"Mum, please don't let him take my babies," she said looking horrified at her father. "Dad, please help me, I can't stay here, if he takes them, they will be frightened, and I'll never see them again."

Her father looked in the direction the car had gone. "If I thought we could get away with it Phyllis, I would take you away tonight, but we could all be prosecuted and then where would Richard and Pauline be, if their parents were in prison, I'm so sorry darling there is nothing we can do."

Phyllis pulled away from her parents. "And what about my children? they will be somewhere they don't know, with people they don't know!" She ran upstairs, she couldn't think what to do, should she run? The children's trunk was packed and hers was almost packed, where could she go, and what if they caught up with her, they would scare the children even more if it happened like that, she was madly trying to figure out what to do, tears were streaming down her face she was a mess, she couldn't think straight, her father was right she had no right to ask them to help her, this was her mess and she had to get herself out of it.

She went downstairs quietly, she looked at her parents, her mother was in tears and her father holding his wife trying to console her.

"I'm sorry, Mum, I'm sorry, Dad I made this mess, it's not your fault at all, I had no right to say those things to you," she said. "I never thought he could be that cruel, and it seems he was planning this before I left, so at least you got to meet your grandchildren."

Winifred hugged her daughter. "I'm so sorry, darling, I wish I had never thought of him as a good father or husband, it's my fault you are in this mess," she said.

They all sat hugging each other on the couch. Freda, Phyllis' younger sister came in with her fiancé, Tom, "What's the matter, why is everyone crying?" she said almost wishing she hadn't asked. "Is it because you are going home, Phil?"

"No that's not it, Freda, my husband is taking my children to a convent in Belgium, they are to board there," Phyllis said tearfully.

"Why Belgium?" she asked.

"I don't know, it's the first I have ever heard of it," Phyllis said.

"Where is it?" Freda asked.

"Bruges," Phyllis replied.

"Is that the English convent?" Freda asked.

"I don't know," Phyllis said. "Still, it would make more sense I didn't know there was an English convent in Belgium."

"Oh yes," Freda went on, "it was used in the seventeen hundreds by Mother Mary More and the exile of the Augustinian canonesses of Bruges in England. We learned that at school," she said. "I didn't know it was still in use, as a school," she continued. "There is a Carrara Marble alter that was donated by the countess of Nithsdale as they helped her husband escape," she laughed, "They dressed him as her lady's maid to get him out of the Tower of London, it was famous," she added.

It all made sense now. Phyllis said, "He's always looking at historic events and kings and queens of England. I'm guessing that's why he wants them to go there, so he can see the convent himself," she said.

"At least we will know where they are," Winifred said, drying her eyes.

"And at least they won't be with him," Phyllis said. "He isn't a good father at all, but I will miss them so dreadfully, I can't possibly go back to India knowing they are in Belgium," she said.

Her father put his hand on her shoulder. "You can stay here as long as you want, Phil. Mum and I will be happy to have you," he said.

Phyllis didn't sleep at all that night she was in the kitchen at six a.m. drinking tea and smoking cigarettes, worrying how she was going to tell the children what their father had planned for them, she knew Megan would cry and worried that Percy would lose his temper with her on the long journey to Belgium. The children got up at seven and they sat at the kitchen table waiting patiently for their breakfast. After they had eaten, Phyllis took them to the lounge and sat them down, she couldn't contain herself, the tears flowed freely down her face.

"What's wrong, Mother?" the children asked.

"Your father came here last night, he has ordered me to have you ready by nine o'clock. He is taking you to a school to board," she said.

Megan started to shake, her face went red and she burst into tears, Owen hadn't understood what his mother had said. "Are we going home?" he asked.

"No," Megan said through her tears. "We are both going away to school, father is taking us. Is it because you disobeyed him, Mother?" She looked accusingly at her mother.

"No, he had planned this even before I decided to come to visit Gran and Grandad. It was lucky I did bring you here, or you would have never met each other," Phyllis said, as she hugged her children.

Owen still hadn't understood properly. "Are you taking us, Mother?" he said, trying to understand why she was crying so much.

"No, my darling boy, your father is taking you on the boat," she said.

"Where is the school?" Megan said, trying to stop crying.

"It's in a country near France, called Belgium. It's an English convent school."

Owen suddenly sat up. "I'm not going," he said. "Father can go to hell!"

Everyone gasped. "Owen, I love that you are so brave but please don't use that language," his mother said softly.

"Why aren't you coming, Mummy?" he said.

"Your father won't let me come, but I will ask him when he comes for you," she said.

Owen got up and ran towards the front door trying to reach the handle, he shouted, "Let me out!"

Megan went to her brother and opened the door. They both ran out of the door and down the street. Just as their father had arrived at the house the children ran as fast as their legs would carry them, "Where are you going, Owen?" Megan cried.

"I don't know," he said, "but I'm not going with Father."

"But we have to, you will get mother into a lot of trouble," she said. He stopped, they were quite far from the house now, Owen looked at Megan

"I don't want to go with Father," he said, trying not to cry, "Megan we won't see Mummy, and I love Mummy."

She took his hand. "I'll take care of you, Owen, I promise," she said. They walked back to the house. "We are ready," she said, looking coldly at her father. "Please wait in your car, Father, we will be out presently."

He started to say something but Cyril stepped in front of the children. "Wait here," he said forcefully. Percy sat in his car, as they both hugged their mother.

"Don't forget me will you, darlings?" she said.

"We will never forget you, Mummy," they promised.

"I will take care of Owen for you," Megan said in her most grown-up voice. "I promise I'll do my best," she said.

Phyllis crumpled onto the floor holding her children, crying loudly, Cyril and Henry were at the front door making sure their father didn't get out of the car, but they could see he was getting impatient.

"I think you better go children. Your father is waiting." Henry was trying his hardest not to cry. He hugged the children and told them to be brave and, "Don't give the blighter the satisfaction of seeing you cry," he said.

Megan hugged her grandmother. "Thank you, for having us, Grandmother," she said kissing her cheek.

"I love you dearly," she said to the small child. "I hope to see you again, darling," she said, as she swapped Megan for Owen.

Cyril picked Megan up and kissed her cheeks. "Don't forget us, darling, we won't forget you, and when you are bigger, come back to us, won't you?" he said.

"When I'm older, Grandad, I'm going to be with my Mummy," she said with a tear in her eye.

He put her down and picked Owen up. "There, there, old man," he said. "Chin up, be a brave little man for Grandad. Remember we love you, and try not to anger your Father. He isn't a good man," he said.

"I hate him," Owen said. "I hate his guts, he's a pig."

Cyril knew that was the worst thing you could ever call someone who was born and raised in India, as pigs were known as the dirtiest and the lowest of the low.

Megan took Owens hand and led him to the car where their

father was waiting, he tried to help the children into the car. Megan just shrugged his hand off her.

"Don't you ever touch me," she said coldly, "We hate you." He got back into the car and drove off forgetting the trunk completely, as it was still sitting in the bedroom.

Phyllis was a mess, she didn't stop crying for days, she didn't come out of her room, her mother took her food on a tray, but she didn't touch any of it. "You must eat Phyllis," she said softly.

"I can't, I've lost my babies, and it would have happened even if I hadn't come to England, he betrayed me," she said. "I will never forgive him. I hate him," she said, crying harder.

"Dad said we could go and take their trunk as he has some holiday days, he has to take," her mother said.

Phyllis sat up. "Can we really?" she said.

"Yes, we can take the ferry over to Ostend and drive to Bruges. Well, they need their things, don't they?" her mother said.

"Yes, I dread to see what those nuns have dressed my babies in," Phyllis said sobbing.

"There, there, dry your eyes, darling," her mother said, giving her a fresh handkerchief.

The next day, Cyril came back from work, he kissed the top of Phyllis's head. "I've got next week off work, we can go to Belgium and see the children."

Winifred kissed her husband. "Thank you, darling," she said softly, he looked at her, she hadn't been this affectionate for years, he knew she felt that it was all her fault. Had she not introduced Percy to Phyllis, this wouldn't be happening, he didn't want to be too hard on his wife as she already was feeling bad about the situation he just smiled and hugged her.

"Don't worry, darling, it will be all right," he said.

The next week dragged on, it felt like time stood still for Phyllis. She had smoked too many cigarettes and drunk too much whisky, she just couldn't face another day without seeing her children, she wondered if they felt as miserable as she did. She worried that they were being treated kindly, she had heard what it was like going to a convent school, she had heard nuns were not very kind people even though they were supposed to be kind, as god was watching their every move. She was angry at Percy for not consulting her about the kind of school he was sending her babies to, what was he thinking sending a three-year-old and four-year-old to boarding school. She ached to hold her darlings. She knew she had to go back to India or she would never know what her children were going through and might never see them again. She had made her mind up she wasn't going back until her brother Errol visited next summer.

She wrote to Percy telling him what her plans were, he wrote back, saying he thought she had left him, that's why he had sent the children when he did, as a punishment, he also said he was sorry, and of course visit your family. He had realised it wasn't such a big thing she had asked for, he didn't know why he had said she couldn't go. But going against his wishes was not acceptable, and she should never have done it. She sat reading the letter. "He wants me to go back," she said to her mother.

Winifred looked at Phyllis "You're not going to, are you?" she said quite shocked that Phyllis would even think of such a thing.

"As you said before, Mum, I can't leave him, I know he would never give me my children, and he would not give me a penny."

"Yes, but darling, if you could get custody of the children, he would have to pay you upkeep."

"But Mum, he is a judge and I'm a woman, maybe in the future, the laws might change but not in time for me and my babies, I would never see them again, I just couldn't bare that." she said trying hard not to cry again today.

She had woken up early crying, she didn't want to cry forever, she was formulating a plan. Percy had said he would write a letter to the reverend mother of the convent, allowing his wife to visit the children, she would never forgive him for what he had done to their children and herself, but at least she would be able to see them, and have them home for holidays.

The day came, it had been weeks since Phyllis had seen her children, she had woken up early feeling a little sick. Winifred had given Richard his clothes and left him to dress himself as she was preparing a picnic luncheon for them to take with them, on the ferry. Henry had gone back to school, so he wasn't going with them, but Richard was going and he was very excited to go on a boat. Cyril had put some blankets in the car just in case they got chilly, and the trunk with the children's clothing in the boot of the car. The sun was out, it was a lovely day. "Have you got everything, passports and such," he asked.

"Yes, dear I have the passports, and I'm not quite sure what the 'and such' is, but I have luncheon, three flasks of tea, and some lemonade for Richard," she said.

"Can I bring my soldiers, Mum?" Richard asked.

"Yes, dear, but please don't lose them." Richard sat smiling in the back seat of the car with his sister.

He looked at Phyllis putting his hand in hers, "It will be all right, Phil, won't it?" he said.

"I hope so," she replied. She was thinking how she could

leave them after seeing them, how would she have the strength to not pick them up and run away with them, she knew she couldn't do that her parents would be implicated and they could be thrown in to prison, thoughts of this had run through her mind for weeks how she could get away with them go somewhere, anywhere, but how she had no money, they would all starve without her parents to help her but she would never ask them it was impossible.

Winifred sat in the front seat straightening her hat, she turned the radio on, there was classical music on. "Oh, Vivaldi," she said smiling, they had an orchestra on the radio station. "Oh, Cyril, do you remember, this was played at the Viscount's Ball in 1927 do you remember?" she said smiling.

"Yes, it is a lovely piece," he said as he drove out of the street. They sat for a moment reminiscing about the old days in India when they were all happy and together.

Cyril had consulted his map and written the route down for Winifred to read out for him. He had never been to Dover before but it was closer to their house than Liverpool. It wasn't long before Richard had fallen asleep with his head resting on Phyllis's lap, just as Owens did months before. Winifred smiled. "He used to love listening to my gramophone records of Mozart and the like," she said smiling.

"I loved music when I was a child too, didn't I mother?" Phyllis said.

Winifred smiled. "You and your brother and sisters used to bother me all the time asking for music on, I remember a time you wouldn't sleep until you had music after your story," she said laughing at the memory she had recalled.

"Dad used to read our bedtime stories, he had such a way of

telling the stories doing all the funny voices," Phyllis recalled.

"Yes, those were such lovely times, I miss having you and Errol and the girls dancing in the parlour. You had the prettiest white dress, I think I had some photographs taken of you in that dress," her mother said smiling.

This reminded Phyllis of the dress she had bought for Megan on her birthday, she would never wear it again as she had left it in India, and by the time she saw her daughter again it wouldn't fit her. It made her think of all the things they had left behind, why did Percy do this? She thought her children were so far from home it would be hard to get more than one visit in a year, she tried hard not to think of all the things that had been going through her mind over the last few weeks, how happy her children were in England and how her family had treated them, they had never had a family before and they didn't have anyone on their fathers side. The only time they were in a situation like that was when they visited the Maharaja, and his wives and children were lovely to them.

Finally, they got to Dover, Cyril got out and purchased the tickets for the ferry, they didn't have to wait very long as the ferry was getting ready to get underway.

"They are going to load the car for us, we have to get on board, this way," Cyril said getting his coat and the luncheon basket. "Are you all right, dear? Do you need a hand?" he said as Winifred got out of the car. She got Richard out from the back seat and Phyllis jumped out as the ship's loader came and took the car to be loaded. "Lucky we could take the car," Cyril said. "If we were any later the next ship is full."

"Where are they taking the car, Dad?" Richard said looking at the big cranes at the side of the dock. "What do they use those for, Dad?" he asked.

"They load train carriages onto the ships with those," his father said, "but that man will drive the car on."

"Oh," Richard said as his mother held his hand and started to walk to the gang-plank. When they were safely onboard, the ship started to move away from the dock, as Phyllis and her parents and brother found a nice comfy seat inside.

"Oh, look dear, we could have got tea on board I needn't have bothered with flasks," she said.

"Yes, but we will need them later so we can drink ours, and when we are due to get off, we can have them filled back up," Cyril said, as they sat eating their luncheon, watching the waves in the channel. It was a lovely day for going on a boat trip, the sea was very calm and it didn't take long until they were docking at Ostend.

"We can drive up to Bruges," Cyril said. "I've got a map in the car, I borrowed it from Bob at work, he goes all the time. We must invite him and his lovely wife over for drinks one night, awfully decent chap," he said, picking up the cups from the flasks he had just had filled up with hot tea. "I don't think we will get back tonight though, do you, dear?" he said looking at the clock on the dockside office.

"Oh, I do hope we do," Winifred said.

"I suppose it depends on how long it takes to get there, doesn't it? I was just talking to a fellow about the ferry, he said that next year you would be able to go on the train from London all the way to Bruges without getting off at all, the train will be loaded on the rails isn't that fascinating?"

"Well, I never," Winifred said. Phyllis was preoccupied she was thinking about her children, she just wanted to hold them, she wanted to take them home and live together, she wished things could have been different. She didn't feel guilty that she had disobeyed her husband, indeed if she hadn't gone, her parents would never have met her children at all, and now they loved her children and she knew they would always be there for them, and that her brother Henry would always have a soft spot for them too.

As they disembarked Cyril had gone on ahead to collect the car, he pulled up in front of them and they got in.

"All right, where's that map?" he said reaching the glove compartment. He pulled out the folded map, opening it out he looked for where they were on the map. "Aha," he said, then folded it to the place where they had to follow. "Can you see, dear, we have to go on that road there." He pointed at the place on the map where they were. "And we need to go to this place here," he said, "Passendale. When we get there, we need to look for signs to Jabbeke, do you see?" he asked.

"Oh, yes, I see," Winifred said.

He nodded and smiled. "I do hope we don't get lost," he said laughing and they set off. Phyllis noticed something wasn't quite right.

"Dad, you are supposed to drive on the other side of the road I think!" she said looking at the other cars.

"Oh yes indeed," her father said blushing slightly, they all laughed.

Phyllis was more excited now, she was going to see her children, they followed the map going past the signs for Passendale and Jabbeke, then onto Sint Andries and onto Sint Anna quarter.

"I do believe this is the street," Winifred said suddenly. "We are here, Carmersstraat."

Cyril pulled up outside a grey building with a dome on top, there was only one door, right on the street, it was a tall wooden door with grey finials above it, Cyril pulled the bell cord. It took quite a while for anyone to come to the door.

"We are here to see Megan and Owen David," Cyril said in a confident voice.

The nun just said, "No, no, monsieur, this is not possible," she went on to ramble on in French, as Phyllis was saying

"I am their mother, these are their grandparents, she simply must let me see my children."

As the grown-ups were arguing Richard slipped into the doorway unseen by the nun and ran down the corridors looking this way and that. He could hear some singing up ahead of him, as he turned a corner he ran into a nun.

"Oh, excuse me," he said forgetting he wasn't in England.

"Why are you out of your class?" the nun said.

Richard looked at the nun thinking fast he said, "I got lost."

The nun thought the child looked familiar and told him to follow her. He did, she opened a classroom door, he immediately saw Megan and Owen sitting in a corner. As he ran over to them, they jumped up hugging him crying.

"How did you get here?" Megan said.

"Mum and Dad are outside, with your Mummy," he said excitedly.

"What is the meaning of this?" the nun who was taking the class said.

"I'm sorry, sister, I thought he was in your class I found him in the corridor," she said, all the other children were staring at them, Richard had similar clothes on as the other children.

Megan, Richard and Owen didn't wait for the nun to stop them, they ran through the classroom door and on to the entrance following close behind were the nuns, shouting, "Children, come back, immediately!"

They didn't listen and kept running, they got to the door just as the other nun was about to close the door in Phyllis's face, she stumbled over as the children ran into her, Richard grabbed the door handle and flung the door open as hard as he could. Owen and Megan tumbled onto the street into their mother's arms as they sat on the floor crying and hugging each other. Phyllis noticed Owen had a bruise on his cheek and jaw.

"Who did this?" she said looking at the bruise. The other nuns had arrived at the door by this time, Cyril stood in front of the children barring the way.

The nun stood speaking very loudly, "If you do not stand aside, sir, I will call a policeman."

Phyllis said, "Go on then, you can explain these bruises on my son's face," she said, hugging her children tightly.

"Madame, ask your husband that question, he arrived here with a bloody nose and those bruises,"

Megan quietly said, "Father hit him because he called him a pig to his face,"

"Yes, I did," Owen said looking very pleased with himself.

"Oh, my baby boy, the brute, how dare he hit you!" Phyllis said hugging her son closely.

"What is the meaning of this?" a voice boomed from behind the doors, the other three nuns looked very anxious and all tried to explain together.

"Reverend Mother, we can explain, these people asked to see Megan and Owen, we didn't see the other little boy, he slipped in unnoticed, I'm so sorry, Reverend Mother." They all apologised at once.

"Who are you, may I ask?" she was looking at Cyril, and Winifred.

"We are their grandparents and this is their mother, they

forgot their trunk and we are bringing them, their clothing," Cyril said.

"There was no need for that," she said looking down her nose at them, "we have a strict uniform policy here, the children won't be wearing their own clothes. Now I will ask you to leave and let the children go back to their classroom," she said coldly.

"Please," Phyllis said. "Please let me see them a while longer, we have come a long way, and they are far too young to be at boarding school, away from me," Phyllis pleaded.

"I'm sorry," the Reverend Mother said, "you must take that up with your husband. You may visit for a while, but not out here in the street, please come into my office."

They all followed the Reverend Mother, and the nuns went back to what they were doing.

"Why are they so quiet?" Richard said to his father.

The Reverend Mother answered, "This is a place of God," she said, "we are silent out of respect."

"Oh," he said, shrugging his shoulders looking at Megan.

"So you haven't come to take us home, Mummy we don't like it here, we want to go home," she said.

"I'm so sorry darling. Your father had decided this is where you will go to school, I am powerless to change his mind, he had ordered me home, I can only hope he can see what he has done and sends for you," Phyllis said.

"I still hate him," Owen said. "He is a pig and I hope he dies."

"Now, now, darling," Phyllis said. "You mustn't say such things, I hope I can persuade him otherwise, we have to be patient, I don't want you here either," she said. All the time thinking to herself I hope he dies too. The Reverend Mother looked at Phyllis. "I'm sorry," Phyllis said, "but I wasn't consulted about sending my children here, and it's very far away from where we live. It was a total shock to us all," she said.

"I understand," the reverend mother said, "I was in contact with your husband last year about sending the children here, I was not aware he didn't say anything to you about it," she said.

"Not to mention it's bally far from us too, we won't see them, it's just not fair!" Richard said stamping his foot.

Cyril tried to ignore Richard's language.

"I want to go home, Mother," Owen said starting to cry.

"Please don't cry, darling, I can't take you home, your father will just send you back and I'll go to prison, then I won't see you at all. I'll try to get father to agree to have you home before Christmas, I promise," Phyllis said trying to keep her composure.

They stayed for an hour but it came time for them to go or they wouldn't make the ferry back to England. Phyllis looked at the Reverend Mother. "I will be back to see them before I return to India. I do hope you allow me to see them," she said sternly.

"I will, Madame," she assured her.

They said their tearful goodbyes again, and left.

"Goodbye, my darlings, don't forget me, will you?" Phyllis said as she left tears flowing down her face.

Megan and Owen ran after her holding on to her skirt they hugged her tightly. "Please don't go, Mother, please," Megan begged her. Owen gripped her skirt tighter all the time crying uncontrollably.

Cyril picked Megan up and gave her a kiss and hugged her close to him, "I wish we could stay, darling, but we have to get back, we will see you soon, I promise."

"Can I come next time, Dad," Richard said trying not to cry too.

"Yes, son you can," his father said.

Richard took two soldiers out of his pocket and gave one to Owen and one to Megan. "We can play with them when we are together again."

Owen took the soldier, "I'll keep it safe, Richard," he said. Cyril gave Megan to Winifred and picked Owen up, he didn't speak he just hugged him close, then gave him to Winifred.

Richard hugged Megan and Owen, "Don't worry, we won't forget you, we promise."

Phyllis gave the children one more hug and let the nuns take the children back into the convent. She could hear them crying from the road as they drove away, it broke their hearts to go, but they had to.

The journey back to Ostend was silent, only the odd sniffle could be heard, Cyril was trying to be strong, but he couldn't imagine leaving one of his children in a foreign country. Even though Jean finished her education in India when they had moved to England but she had been at that school for years before they moved and she was at the end of her schooling not three or four years old.

"What will you do now, Phil?" he said as they boarded the ship home.

"I'll stay with you until Errol visits, then I'll go back to India, I have to try to change Percy's mind and get my children out of that place," she said.

"What if he doesn't change his mind?" Winifred said frowning.

"Then I will have to try to visit them as often as I can and try to get them home for Christmas at least," she said.

They arrived home after dark, Winifred put Richard straight to bed. "That was a lovely thing you did today, Richard, I know how much you love your soldiers," she said as she tucked him in bed.

"Well, they are alone, and I didn't want them to be," he said.

Phyllis and her father sat in the lounge drinking as they had done many times since Phyllis arrived. "I think you are very brave going back, Phil," Cyril said sipping his whisky.

"I have no choice, Dad, if I don't go back, I will lose my children forever, and he will have won."

Winifred came in just as Phyllis had finished saying, "What has he won? You will have left him, and his children are thousands of miles away," she said.

"He never cared much for the children, Mum, I wonder if he really cared for me, the way he treats me, but he did say he sent the children away because he thought I had left him," she said.

"Just makes me think he's nothing but a cad!" Cyril said emptying his glass. "Well, I'm off to bed now, it's been a long day," he said.

"Sleep well, Dad," Phyllis said.

"Oh, I doubt I will sleep, dear, but I'll try," he said leaving the room. "Good night, dears," he said as he climbed the stairs.

Winifred looked at her daughter. "I don't think he will be all right about this for a long time, he does love you all so much."

"Yes, I know," Phyllis said. "I don't think he understands any more than I do why anyone could do that to children," Phyllis added.

"No, it's not something anyone with normal sensibilities could understand," Winifred said. "I'm making some cocoa, do you want some?" she said as she went to the kitchen.

"No thanks, Mum, I'm going to finish this and go to bed myself, I'm exhausted." With that she drained her glass and went to bed. She didn't think she would sleep either. She lay tossing and turning most of the night, sleep only found her in the early hours, and then she slept most of the next day away. When she finally came downstairs her mother was reading in the lounge, and Richard was in the garden playing with his remaining soldiers.

"Where's Dad?" she asked her mother.

"You two are so alike. Where do you think he is?" she said smiling.

Phyllis thought, and then said, "Well, if we are alike, he's still in bed."

"No," her mother said, "he has been up for about an hour, he didn't sleep until about four a.m., then he didn't wake up till late afternoon," Winifred said.

"So where is he now?" Phyllis asked

"He just went to get an evening paper," Winifred said, "Dinner will be in an hour. The girls will be home soon."

"I'm sorry, Mum, I should have got up before now and helped with Richard," Phyllis said.

"Oh no, that's all right dear," her mother said tapping her hand. "Richard keeps himself happy until he needs food, and I've been reading most of the day, it's been quite quiet," she said.

"I think I'll get a job," Phyllis said. "I was thinking to myself earlier."

"A job? What on earth for?" her mother said.

"Yes, I'm quite a good secretary," Phyllis said. "I do like to be the boss usually, but I'm sure I will manage, I'm nearly out of cash, and I don't want Percy to have yet another hold over me," she said.

Cyril came into the living room with his paper. "Oh, there you are dears," he said. "Sleep well?" he asked.

"Yes," Phyllis said. "I slept a little more than I should have, but I feel better for it."

He turned to Winifred. "I'm sorry I overslept, dear, it must have been a nightmare trying to sleep in the same room as me last night."

Winifred waved her hand at him. "Oh, don't worry about me," she said. "I've had a really quiet day of it here to make up for your tossing and turning," she laughed.

"Can I see that paper when you have finished with it?" Phyllis said, pointing at the newspaper in her father's hand.

"Yes, of course, looking for anything particular?" he asked.

"She says she's going to get a job," her mother interjected.

"A job?" Cyril said.

"Yes, if I'm not going home until after the summer I might as well get a job, I can't just stay here and not give you housekeeping," she said.

"Well, there is a job going at my place, just an office junior, but it will be all right for a while," her father said. "I'll give Bob a ring, if you like," he said smiling at his daughter.

"Oh, would you, Dad, that would be fabulous."

The next day, Cyril set up an interview for Phyllis for the following week. During that time Phyllis went shopping with her sister Kitty and bought a very nice suit and a silk blouse to go with it. Of course, she wrote a cheque for it as it was very expensive, she thought Percy at least owed her that. She wrote to him telling him that she would be visiting the children in a month or two and that she had booked her passage home.

He wrote back saying, "Take your time, I'll have your room decorated for your return."

She thought, *that would be nice, but you won't see inside it until you give me my children back you cad.* She would make him pay for taking her babies away. She may be going back, but she would not perform her wifely duties.

The interview was quite straight-forward, and Phyllis was hired there and then.

"When can you start?" Bob said to her.

"Well as soon as possible," she answered.

"Good, I'll see you bright and early in the morning," he said as he shook Phyllis's hand vigorously.

Phyllis took tea in a lovely café around the corner from her father's workplace as she waited for him to finish work.

"How did it go?" he asked when he arrived at the café.

"Good," she said, "I start in the morning."

"Oh, good," he said, as he drove them home.

Phyllis's mind strayed to her children often over the next few months, she wrote to them often, but never got a reply, she made her mind up to visit them at Christmas. She wrote to the Reverend Mother telling her of her plans, but the reply she got was that she wouldn't be able to visit, until her husband had given his permission.

She immediately wrote to Percy asking for permission. He wrote back telling her he didn't think it was wise, as the children were very upset the last time she visited, but he did say when she had returned to India, she would be able to have the children home for visits. Phyllis didn't bother to write back to Percy as she knew she was flogging a dead horse, he wouldn't change his mind, and if she couldn't see the children, there was little point in her visiting them and wondered if they had even received her letters.

Phyllis enjoyed working for her father's firm and was saving every penny she could. Christmas came and went, she didn't come out of her room on Christmas Day, she couldn't face the merriment without her children. She didn't want to ruin everyone else's day by being miserable around the rest of the family. She left gifts under the tree for everyone, and wrote lovely notes to the family, thanking them for their unwavering support over the last few months. Still, Phyllis couldn't face it, not without her Meg and Owen, she wondered if they were having a lovely time, but she guessed they were not. How could they, they were in a place without anyone that cared for them, no presents, nothing. She had sent some gifts for them but guessed they wouldn't receive them, just like her letters. She still sent a letter every week in the hope that some kind soul deemed to give the children her words of courage and love. She had been in England a year now, she worked hard and saved harder, she didn't know what she was going to do, as her plans were not panning out and she didn't want to return to India. She hated that she had even met Percy, she hated him with all her heart, he had successfully destroyed her life and that of her children, they were alone in a country that didn't even speak English, she ached to hold them, but it was futile.

Unless she returned to India after her brother's visit, she knew she would never see her darlings again.

The months rolled on, and the family were looking forward to Errol and Jessie visiting, with their two little boys, that Phyllis had heard so much about, her mother adored them. At last, they had arrived, the whole family were at home now all, but Meg and Owen. Phyllis felt it even more now her brother will never meet them, the thought of that left Phyllis so desperately sad. Errol hugged his little sister and said how sad he was to hear about her children.

"I missed you," he said quietly. Jessie had her hands full of her youngest son, William, she was holding Cyril's hand. Phyllis knelt down in front of Cyril and hugged the small boy, he smiled at her and said hello in a broad Scottish accent, Phyllis laughed, William was laughing too, he liked laughing. Jessie gave the small child to Phyllis to hold, Phyllis smiled for the first time in ages, she hadn't held a baby since Owen was born, it felt good, and the child seemed to be happy all the time, how could anyone be sad around such happiness.

They posed for the obligatory photos, Errol always had his camera, he said with a family as big as ours it's easy to forget things and pictures helped to remember. With that Phyllis ran upstairs she couldn't hold in her tears any longer, she didn't have any pictures of her babies. They were all at home in India, and she didn't take any of them when they arrived, as she had no idea this was going to happen. How she missed them.

Errol and Jessie stayed for a week, it was the hight of summer the weather was wonderful, they went to London zoo the children had so much fun looking at the elephants and gorillas, Errol told stories of the elephants in India the children marvelled at the monkeys, they had picnics in Hyde park watching people sailing little boats on the lake, just before the end of the week they took the children to the tower of London, Pauline particularly liked the gruesome history of Anne Boleyn and the missing princes, Richard and Cyril climbed onto a canon Errol took lots of photographs as he always did. As they got back home everyone went about sorting themselves out, but try as she may Phyllis couldn't stop thinking about her children how they would have loved the outings and spending time with their cousins, she tried to remember their giggles, alas nothing came to her but tears, she tried to hide her grief but Errol was watching her, he put his arm around her shoulder and hugged her. "I'm so sorry, Phil," he said.

"Oh, don't mind me," she said trying to put on a brave face. "I'll be fine, you'll see."

"I hope so," he replied.

"It's been a long day," she said. "I'm off to bed. I'll see you in the morning.

The next day the children were making so much noise they were sent to play in the garden, Errol and Jessie were sorting out the car for the journey home, the time had flown by very quickly, it was time to leave, it was a sad day, saying goodbye. They all hugged and kissed each other, took some last moment pictures and off they went. With the rest of the family waving until they were out of sight, they sadly went back inside the house, feeling deflated.

"I suppose I have to make arrangements to leave too," Phyllis said, as they closed the front door.

"Yes, I suppose," Winifred said looking very sad.

"Are you really going back to India, Phil?" Henry said, looking concerned.

"I have to, Henry, or I'll never see my children again, if I don't," she said downheartedly.

"You don't have any guarantee you will see them even if you do go back," he retorted. "That cad doesn't know the meaning of keeping his word, he doesn't see you as his wife just someone who he had children with and took them away. He's a cruel man, and I don't understand why you would go back to him!" he said angrily.

"I'm not going back for my health, Henry, he will never touch me again," she said forcefully. "I just have to try to get my children back, and this is the only way. Trust me he will regret the day he ever clapped eyes on me, I hate him."

Phyllis sat in the lounge as she watched Richard play, he

stopped and smiled at her. "I'm going to miss you when you go, Phil, won't you stay please?" he said holding her hand.

"I can't stay here, Richard, I have to try to get Megan and Owen back. I promise I'll come back and see you."

"Will you, really?" he said, content with that he went back to playing. "I would like that very much," he said. She sat looking at the small boy who looked so much like her children; she hoped when she came back, it was with them in tow.

The day came when Phyllis packed her things. Her father was preparing to take her to Liverpool, to the ship that would take her back to India, she hugged her mother goodbye. Henry was back at school, and she had said goodbye to him the day before, he was still angry that she was going back but understood why. Her younger sisters Jean and Freda came to say goodbye; as she hugged them Richard tugged on her skirt

"I've made you a card, Phil, to look at while you're on the boat home." He gave her an envelope she took the card out and read it: Dearest Phil, I will miss you, please come back soon, love from your brother, Richard. She held it to her heart.

"Thank you, darling," she said and hugged him close, he looked very sad as her father drove away. Phyllis wasn't looking forward to going back, but she knew she had to. The car journey was very quiet her father looked deep in thought. "I know what you're thinking, Dad," she said, "but I have to go."

"I can't talk right now, Phil," he said, his face went red, and he had to pull over, he reached for his handkerchief and blew his nose. "I'm sorry, dear, I didn't mean to let you see that," he said.

She put her hand on his, "Don't worry, Dad, I'll be fine and if I'm not, I'll come straight back, I promise," she said patting his hand.

"I hope you will, darling," her father said. "I hate that you have to return to that cad, but I do understand why you must try. There is nothing more important than family," he said. "And little Meg and Owen shouldn't have to be in that awful place, alone."

The ship was in the dock when they got to Liverpool, Phyllis sighed a big sigh, pulling herself up she got out of the car taking her trunk. She had left her children's trunk at her parents as she didn't see the point in bringing their things all the way back to India when they weren't going to be there. She had her trunk loaded and hugged her father.

"I love you, Phil, don't forget, will you?" he said.

"No, Dad, never," she replied. "I love you too, and thank you for all you have done for me. I really appreciate it."

"It was nothing," he said, giving her one last hug.

She turned and walked up the gang-plank to the ship that would take her home.

The journey felt too short, and before she knew it, she was getting off the ship in Bombay, she felt the warm air on her skin and the smell of spices filled her nostrils, it had a comforting feel, she did love India, but she also knew she wasn't staying. As soon as she could convince Percy to let her have her children back, she would leave with them as soon as they reached an age where he had no say in their lives. She would never let him touch her again, she couldn't risk having another child to this man, he was cruel and heartless, and he didn't deserve her love or that of her children.

As the taxi brought her nearer to the house she had shared with her husband and children just over a year ago, the memories of that time flooded back, she felt the tears roll down her cheeks, she quickly checked herself and wiped the tears away with her handkerchief, she would shed no more tears, this is a time of revenge, and there was no room for sentiment.

She had the taxi driver put her trunk in her room and paid him for his troubles, and she was relieved that Percy was away and wouldn't be back for three days according to the servant who opened the door for Phyllis. She looked pleased to see her, even though Phyllis wasn't smiling, she was happy to see the staff hadn't changed, the cook wasn't there, in the kitchen was a new cook.

"What happened to Annie?" she asked. Percy always gave his staff English names when they arrived in his household, he didn't like Indian names and wouldn't allow them to use them.

"She was let go, memsahib," the new cook said. "The master asked her where you went, she didn't answer him so, he let her go."

Phyllis knew Annie well, she had always hidden her secrets, the deserts she provided her children and any other things Phyllis didn't want Percy to know about.

"Fired, poor thing," Phyllis said, she knew where Annie's family lived and made a note to go to see her when she got settled in.

The house hadn't changed much in the year Phyllis was gone except her bedroom, it had a new coat of rose-pink paint, and the curtains had been changed along with the bedding. At least Percy had good taste, she thought, she went to her chest to see if he had touched her things, he hadn't.

After she had unpacked her trunk she went to the nursery, she smelled her children in there, the soap they used was in the bathroom, she picked up the teddies she had bought for them the Christmas before they had left, she sat on the floor and wept clinging to the bears as though she were clinging to them.

The housemaid came into the room, she quietly sat beside Phyllis.

"Where are they?" she said softly, Phyllis turned to the servant it was the same ayah that she took to the mountains the summer before they left.

"He has put them where I can't see them," she said tearfully. "They are in a convent in another country."

The servant looked away. "He is a cruel man," she said.

"Yes," Phyllis nodded. "I didn't know how cruel before, but now I know," she said bitterly.

She got up and started to pile the toys up, she opened a chest that was in the corner.

"I can't look at these any longer. I think I will send them to England to my parent's house," she said. The servant helped Phyllis put all the children's toys in the chest, then retrieved her own trunk and proceeded to put all the children's clothing in it. Phyllis stopped to smell them before putting them in the trunk, finally there was nothing left in the nursery that reminded her of her absent children. She called a shipping company to collect the things and posted them to her parents, along with photographs that she just couldn't look at. There were no pictures of her children in any other room in the house except her bedroom. She put them all in the trunk.

She asked the gardener who decorated her bedroom.

"I did, memsahib," he said.

"Could you possibly paint this room for me, my children won't be needing this room, and I cannot stand to look at it any longer," she said trying very hard not to cry in front of the staff.

The next day the gardener started to paint the walls. Everywhere Phyllis looked she saw her children, the part of the garden they loved to dig in the mud, the porch they sat on with her, reading nursery rhymes and every night she cried herself to sleep, even in her sleep she heard them cry for her waking her from her slumber. She made sure her door was locked every night, even though Percy was away, he had a habit of coming home when she least expected him to, well he won't be coming into my room she thought to herself, he will never touch her, not until he agreed to give her the children back.

On the third day she came down to the kitchen for breakfast, the cook was preparing breakfast for the master.

"Is he here?" Phyllis whispered.

"Yes, memsahib," the cook replied. "He will take his food in the study," she said.

Phyllis sat at the kitchen table and ate her food, then she left the house and went to the overseas club, where she was meeting with her dear friend and cousin Cynthia who was visiting her parents Tom and Eve, her father's brother and sister-in-law. Cynthia lived in Calcutta but was spending some time with her parents, as they too had decided to move to England, their other daughter Norah had already gone, they thought it was the right time to go too. As she sipped her tea relaying tearfully to her uncle and aunt and cousin what her husband had done, they sat looking in horror,

"Why?" Tom said. "Why on earth would someone do that to their own children?"

"I was looking forward to seeing them this summer," Eve said tearfully. "I found some lovely material and was going to make Meg a dress, but I'm guessing they don't get mail from anyone if he has stopped mail from their own mother," she said.

"That's probably right, he even stopped me saying goodbye when I returned to India," she said.

"The bounder!" Tom said. "I should go over immediately and give him a piece of my mind," he said, half getting up.

"There is no need," Phyllis said putting her hand on his. "He will get his karma, I don't know when, but he will," she said, "and there is no knowing what he is capable of doing to anyone who interferes," she said. "Oh, Dad sends his love," she said trying to change the subject.

"How are your parents?" he said. "Keeping well I hope?"

"Yes, very well, and I'm sure they would love for you to visit when you move."

"Oh, yes, we would too, I haven't seen Cyril since 1931, they did send us a card last Christmas but I'm damned if I know where I put it, it had their address on it," Tom said.

"I thought they would go to Canada with Errol," Eve said.

"Yes, they did go and see him, but he moved to Scotland with his wife to her parents. Mum and Dad moved to Surrey," Phyllis said. "They said it was a trifle cold in Scotland for them."

"I've heard its very nice in Surrey," Tom said. "And of course, Uncle Rivers lives there too."

"Yes, I liked it very much, I really didn't want to come back but I had to you see, any chance I have of changing Percy's mind I have to take," Phyllis said, getting ready to leave the club. She gave her aunt and uncle a hug and walked out with Cynthia,

"What are you going to do?" she said.

"Nothing," Phyllis said. "I'll cry and wail every night and lock my bedroom door," she said. "He will never lay a hand on me again," she said with conviction. "I'll make him regret the day he took my babies away from me," she said.

As Phyllis entered her house, Percy was in the drawing-room "Good trip?" he said trying to strike up a conversation.

Phyllis looked at him, she was trying very hard not to bite, she must retain her composure, all she could muster up was, "I'm going to my room, I have a headache." With that she disappeared.

He carried on listening to the radio acting as though she had been there all along and had not been away for over a year. Phyllis closed her bedroom door and locked it leaving the key in the lock so he couldn't get in, she knew he had another set of keys made, as the key that was there before she left was markedly different. She went to her bathroom and took a warm bath with scented oils and retired to bed. During the night she heard the door handle rattle, he couldn't get in she smiled to herself, he will never get in, she thought, he went away, and she fell asleep.

The next day Phyllis went to Annie's home, the little house was empty, she asked what had happened to the family who lived there. The next-door neighbour told her they had been evicted and had to return to their parent's house in the next town. Phyllis couldn't help feeling sorry for Annie, but there was very little she could do.

The years passed and Phyllis carried on as though Percy was someone else's husband, not hers. She never spoke to him, never ate at the same table as him and never let him in her room at any time. Her uncle and aunt along with most of her cousins had moved to England, she would see them again she hoped.

It was 1939, there was talk of war. Phyllis was distraught, she asked Percy what he was going to do, he asked her what she was talking about.

"My children," she said almost screaming at him, "my children are in Belgium. There is a war starting," she screamed.

"Don't be ridiculous," he said, "there is no war starting!"

"Yes, there is, Germany has invaded Poland and France has declared war on Germany. You must get my children out of there," she screamed.

"I'm not talking to you if you scream at me," he said

pompously, he got up and went out saying, "You imagine things, Phyllis."

Percy had heard there was a world war starting, he had already had the children moved to England to a boarding school in Buckinghamshire, but he didn't want Phyllis to see that he had done this. Phyllis was frantic she went to Percy's study and went through his desk she found the paperwork for the boarding school Bayfield High School, Little Brick Hill in Newport Pagnell in Buckinghamshire. She quickly wrote down the address and left the room making sure nothing was disturbed. She was relieved that they were not in Belgium any longer as she imagined it wasn't a very nice place. She wrote to her parents telling them where the children were, as it was coming up to Christmas. She was hoping this school would allow gifts for the children, she sent some gifts via the army post, she had several friends on the army base in New Delhi. Still, she wouldn't know if the children received them for months.

She wrote to her parents telling them where the children were, she hoped they could visit them at their earliest convenience. Her parents wrote back saying that they had visited the children and they were safe, but didn't remember them at all, but they had received her gifts, and they also wrote that Henry had enlisted in the army. Phyllis read the letter over and over and thought to herself if they have forgotten Mum and Dad maybe they have forgotten me too she thought tearfully, and wondered how they could have forgotten them in such a small amount of time, four years was but a little amount of time to an adult but she thought to a child it must have been so long. She asked Percy to have the children returned to India for their safety, but he refused.

"They are fine where they are," he said, not even looking at Phyllis.

"You are a cad, sir," she said, "a cad! I wish I had never clapped eyes on you," she said as she ran to her room crying uncontrollably. Percy didn't care what she thought, he cared about his children in his own way, but he wasn't the kind that showed affection easily. He had written to his children telling them how their mother didn't care for them and she was very happy without them, the worst thing about this is they believed him. They had never received a single letter from their mother in all the years they were away at school and she promised to see them before she went back to India, and according to their father, she was already in India with him. He would never tell them he forbade her to see them, and made sure they never received the letters and presents their mother had sent them. They had received some presents, they thought they were from mother. The people who came to see them told them that they were their grandparents and said the presents were from their mother, this confused them,

"But father said she didn't want to see us," Owen said to Megan. He didn't remember them, but he did remember the soldier that Richard gave him. He kept it safe, he didn't remember why he valued it so much, but he did still have it. Owen became very jaded he would never speak of his mother, Megan, however sad it made her, did believe her father, but she had received the gifts from her mother, she was a child she had no idea how powerful men were, and that women had no rights in such things. She didn't know that her father was a powerful man and Phyllis had no say about anything pertaining to the children's lives and her marriage.

One day they will know, Phyllis said to herself, I hope they will know what I've tried to do for them, and remember how loved they were when they were small and in the care of their mother.

Phyllis wrote to her parents regularly, but they would not be able to visit the children again as Percy had given strict instruction to the Head they were not to visit. He hadn't said this to the head before as he didn't know that Phyllis knew where they were. He had received a letter from the Head telling him the children had had visitors and who they said they were. He wasn't happy, but there was nothing he could do after the event, he did write to the children telling them those people are nothing to do with them, and they are liars and thieves. He didn't want them to be hurt by them so had forbidden them to visit again.

Megan read her father's letters, she was very upset, she tried so hard to remember but she just couldn't. Owen didn't try he was very angry, the children didn't get visitors, not even their own parents came to see them. if there wasn't a war going on the other children would go home to their parents and Megan, and Owen never got to go home. Owen felt unloved and alone except for Megan, she was always there for him, she had promised she would never leave him.

The war carried on, and Phyllis did what she could for the war effort, she kept herself busy. But she couldn't stop thinking about her children, although, she was happy they were safe, and in England, but the fact they had forgotten her made her very sad. She never let Percy visit her room and swore she would never give in to his bullying tactics, he had ruined her life and her children's, she never spoke to Percy about the children again — what would be the point, he would never tell the truth.

It was late September 1941, Phyllis was getting ready to go

out, she had bought a new dress and had her hair done, she looked like a film star.

"Where are you going looking like that?" Percy said with a sneer.

"I've been invited to the Viscount's Ball," she said. "You remember, you had an invite too, but you said you didn't want to go. Well, I'm going with Uncle Tom and Aunt Eve, it's Cynthia's last week in Delhi as she is moving to England. This will be her last engagement, she has a very well-paid job in England, personal assistant to some Sir, something in the House of Commons," she said. The truth was Cynthia was going to the Ball, but her parents had long gone to England. Percy lied to her constantly so she decided what's sauce for the goose and all that.

A hoot came from the street outside the house and Phyllis grabbed her bag and left. She had a wonderful time dancing the night away with her cousin, she got a little tipsy but she didn't want Percy to know she had had too much to drink or it would be yet another thing she had done wrong in his eyes. She opened the front door very quietly, one of the servants was there to help her to her room, but Percy had stayed up for her and waved the servant away. As they were left alone in the front hall, he asked her if she had had fun, she replied him with a smile.

"I was thinking, we should have the children home for Christmas," he said.

Phyllis was overjoyed she looked at him with a stunned look on her face "Really Percy, do you mean it?" she said.

"Yes, why not?" he said smiling, as he went back to the drawing-room, she skipped to her room totally forgetting to lock the door.

When she had been in bed for a short time thinking about seeing her darlings, she drifted off to sleep dreaming of her beloved children. Later on, that night, Percy opened the bedroom door and got into her bed. Phyllis awoke, but wasn't really thinking about what he was doing she was drunk and happy as she thought she would be seeing her babies. Percy wasn't a kind man, he had no intention of sending for the children he just wanted to visit Phyllis's bed, he took what he wanted and left the room.

In the morning when Phyllis awoke, she remembered what he had done the night before, she was bruised, and in pain, she had the servant draw a bath, and she relaxed into it, sobbing in pain, and hoping he didn't get her pregnant. She still hated Percy, but the thought she was seeing her children for Christmas kept her from falling apart.

As she ate her breakfast in the dining room, Percy came into the room.

"Sleep well?" he asked.

"Somewhat," she said remembering the pain she still felt from his roughness. "I'm going shopping today for the children. I can't wait for Christmas." she said smiling.

"What are you talking about?" he said, "the children won't be coming home this year."

She looked at him totally destroyed. "Why did you tell me they were coming home?" she said hardly believing her ears.

"I never said they were coming home," he said.

"Yes, you did," she screamed.

"If you are going to scream at me, I'll be going out for lunch," he said.

"Go out, who cares!" she shouted. "You are a disgusting disgrace of a man!"

"Disgusting!" he shouted. "Who was it coming in so late stinking drunk? You are the disgrace!" he said and left the room.

Phyllis sat at the table, she couldn't hold back the tears, she really thought her children were coming home. She finished eating and went to her room, she couldn't see through the mist of anger and upset. She thought about leaving, but where would she go? Yes, her father had said she could go there anytime but she was a big girl and could fight her own battles, couldn't she? She decided to stay for a little while longer as she thought only babies go running to mother when things get tough. She knew now that Percy would never change his mind about bringing her children back to India.

The weeks went on, she didn't even try to speak to Percy, she wouldn't speak to him again she thought to herself. Later that week he went away for a few weeks, she decided to write to her sister.

"My Dearest Kitty

I hope this letter finds you well and happy, Mother wrote to me last week, she says you and Mervyn are taking the children and moving to Australia after the war has ended. Be sure to pop in for a visit on the way won't you. I miss you so much and feel quite like a prisoner here. I went to the house in Lahore for the summer, alone of course, as I can't spend more than a few minutes in the same room as Percy. I took just two servants as he wanted the others to stay at home, he said he needed them, but I'm sure it was to make my life harder. I spent some time at the club, there were more familiar faces there than I thought there was going to be, as some were visiting from England. Do you remember the Commander? Well, he was there with his sons who were visiting him. They moved with their mother to England three years ago, they are really getting on well after going to Cambridge. They own a large Insurance company, they said I could have a job anytime, I think they were joking, but if I return to England, I will definitely look them up.

Percy was quite amicable last week he even spoke of having the children home for Christmas, but it was just a ploy to visit my bed. The next day he denied saying anything of the sort. Kitty, I'm drowning here, I miss my babies and my family, I am at a loss as to what to do. Percy is so cold and controlling. Why on earth did I let mother, talk me in to marrying such a man? He often taunts me saying if I leave, I will never see my children again, but Kitty I haven't seen them in five years. I tried to visit them in Belgium before I left for India, but they wouldn't let me in, let alone see them. Percy left strict instructions that I shouldn't see them, how could he be so cruel?

I'm broken, I cannot be mended. Divorce is unthinkable, Percy's a judge, who will represent me who isn't afraid of him destroying their own career? Anyway, I have no money of my own, he controls everything, I can't leave, where would I go? I can't drag Mum and Dad into my marital disharmony again. I tried that, and we all know how that turned out. No one would want me after this, I'm ruined. I sometimes think the only way out is to end it all, please don't mention this at all to mother, I'm too coward to kill myself, don't worry dearest Kitty. I'm so glad you have a kind husband, love your children and keep safe.

All my love
Phyllis XXXXXX

That night she dressed and went to the club, she had so many friends there, Cynthia could only stay a short time, as she was catching the ship from Bombay in the morning and she didn't want to miss it.

Phyllis stayed quite late as she wasn't going anywhere, even though her original plan was to change Percy's mind and bring her children home, this had not happened.

"You look all forlorn," said a smooth manly voice behind her, she turned around to see who was talking to her. It was an old college friend, George. "Can I buy you a drink?" he said, "then you can tell me all about it," he smiled.

Phyllis smiled for the first time that day, she agreed to have a drink with him. They sat at a small table in the corner.

"Now then," he said, "what's the long face for?" Phyllis didn't usually tell her woes to anyone except her closest friends and family, but he had a kind face and she remembered he was a kind boy back in the days when she attended college.

Phyllis went to an all-girl school, she attended a small college learning office duties as she wanted to work in the overseas club and needed some training. George was on the same course, he was going to be a journalist, but that went by the board when the war started and he ended up in the army. He looked very nice in uniform she thought to herself, she spent the evening telling George all about it, he couldn't believe it. "Why on earth did you marry such a bounder?" he said. "Oh, I'm sorry Phil, I shouldn't have said that." he said.

"No, no, I know who he is," she said, "and I have asked myself that same question over and over and still haven't come up with the answer," she said almost in tears. "But now I'm finished trying to get him to change his mind, I think I'm going to leave him and go to England, I was there for a year when this all happened and I loved it apart from not having my children of course, but if I'm not to have them until they are of an age to choose, I might as well leave the curmudgeon, and have some happiness while I'm young, even though I'm thirty-five next year," she said.

"Yes, you should go have yourself a little life before you can legally have your children back."

Suddenly Phyllis was sad again, she had just remembered that the children had forgotten her, she would have to help them remember she thought, and smiled again.

Phyllis started to meet George often at the club. They forged a strong friendship, nothing more, it could never be as George was a married man, his wife was in England and had no plans of moving back to India, George was an officer in the army, and Phyllis was a virtuous woman, she had every reason not to be faithful, but she valued her reputation and liked it that other people thought she was a good woman. It was hard to be faithful to such a cruel man, but she never strayed.

The weeks went on and Phyllis knew her period was due a week before, she couldn't be pregnant she thought, but just in case the servants were on his side she took some of the blood from a chicken that was slaughtered that morning and put it in the sink with her undergarments to make it look like she had come on during the night. She kept her menstrual cycle to herself and never let the staff wash her underclothes so it wasn't obvious, and she wasn't on for long, she pretended to dispose of her towels in the incinerator as usual and didn't draw anyone's attention to her, she made sure her door was locked and bolted at night he would never touch her again. She missed two periods and started to panic, she told George she thought she was expecting, he had grown very fond of Phyllis and told her not to worry.

"You will have to make a plan of how you will leave, pack your things as if you were clearing out your closet for new things, pretend to sell things and when you are ready tell him you are pregnant with another man, he will throw you out of the house and you will be free to go to your parents," he said.

She sat thinking. "Yes, but George who will I say is the

father?" She knew that plan was terribly floored.

"Easy, say I'm the father," he said. She looked at him.

"Don't be ridiculous," she said, "he will have you thrown out of the army and disgraced, I could never tell him you are the father," she said.

"Well, don't tell him anything then, just say he is not the father. He would have been told of the blood in your sink, and he will know he hasn't touched you after that, so let him wonder. Anyway, how do you know when you were in England, he didn't take a mistress," he said.

"I don't," she said frowning.

"Well then, there you are," he said. "If you move your belongings out gradually and send them to England, of course, you have no guarantee that they will get there as it's a perilous thing getting to England during this awful war," he said. "Have you thought about how you will get to England, you can't wait till the end of the war you will have had the baby and where would you stay," he said.

"Yes, you are quite right, he will cut me off without a penny, and I can't have the baby here, he will know it's his," she said.

"Don't you think maybe it would be better to stay and have the baby here?" George said.

"No, I can't, he will take my child away just like he did before," she said almost crying. "I can't let him know it's his baby. George please can't you come up with something? I would rather die than give him another of my children," she begged.

"Let me think on it, Phil, I know some people, just get your things together and start to syphon money," he said.

"Syphon?" she said questioningly.

"Yes, you will need some money to live on while you are pregnant and you will need baby things, clothing you know," he said. "I can help you and I'm sure my sister can put you up for a while," he said.

"Yes, yes, I see," she said. "Oh, are you sure? That would be wonderful," she said.

"Make sure that you leave nothing you value as he won't let you come back to get it," he said. George had the measure of this curmudgeon his dear friend had married he hated seeing her suffer so,

"I know," she said, "but I have to do this, I can't lose another child to him."

He looked at her. "No, I understand," George said putting his hand on hers. "Don't worry, Phil, I'll find out if you can get on an escort carrier. They go to England all the time taking food and uniforms and the likes to England."

Phyllis smiled weakly, "I better go," she said, "it's getting late and thank you, George, for all your helpful advice I really appreciate it," she said.

She turned and left the club, her mind buzzing, she couldn't think straight, did I really mean I would die before I gave Percy another child of mine? She thought. If I go on a ship to England, I could be killed, but at least he wouldn't get his hands on you my darling she said, resting her hand on her stomach.

Over the next week Phyllis pretended to sell her prized possessions, her desk that her father had bought her, some lovely chairs she had in her bedroom, she packed all of her summer clothes and sent them all to England. I hope they get there she thought, she had received a letter from her mother saying the two trunks she had sent had arrived, and the children's toys and clothing she had sent when she arrived back in India, they had put it all in the attic. Phyllis knew there couldn't be much room left in her parents attic, Phyllis sat down to write her mother back she told her she was sending her desk and chairs and two more trunks and hoped they could store them for her while she got ready to leave Percy. She thanked them fervently for their unfailing support expressing how much she appreciated and loved them. She had been taking money out of the bank slowly and changing it into pounds, she packed a small bag of essentials, happy that she had everything and enough money to survive for a good, few months.

She waited for Percy to come home, he had been away, so it was very easy to get her things out without him noticing. Percy was in the study as usual, she walked in without knocking, much to Percy's annoyance. She sat on the edge of the desk he sat up and stared at her

"What are you doing?" he asked.

She looked at him down her nose just like he did to her when he was being nasty, "Well, Percy," she said, "I think I'm going to make this easy for you. I'm leaving you, I'm in love with someone else and we are having a baby, so I'm guessing you will want a divorce," she said, making out she didn't have a care in the world.

He was struggling to keep his temper. "What do you mean you're having a baby?" he said in disbelief.

"Just as I said, I'm in love with another man and we are having a baby, I will be going now," she said, and promptly got off the desk and walked towards the door.

Percy jumped up cutting her escape off. "You can't leave me," he shouted.

"Oh, on the contrary, I can," she said.

He didn't stop her leaving as she pushed past him with a smile and walked to the corner of the street where George's sister, Dora, was waiting in her car. She drove away as soon as Phyllis got into the car. She had made arrangements to stay with Dora, until George had sorted out her travel arrangements to England, it wasn't a problem her staying with Dora as her husband was in the army too and wasn't at home at the present. George stayed with Dora on occasion as she hated being alone and with her husband away, she welcomed the company. Dora and her husband were planning on going to England when he retired from the army, so Phyllis would tell her all about living in England as Dora was born and raised in Madras and had never been out of the country at all. Of course, she had read a lot about England and was very interested about the history, but Phyllis was there for over a year and she was able to tell her about her experience. They soon became firm friends.

A few days later George came back from the army base, he told Phyllis of a convoy that was due to leave from Bombay the following week, it was going straight to England it was carrying a cargo of uniforms and food, and he had made sure the ship she would be on had a good doctor so she would be in good hands.

"Oh, George I don't know how to thank you," she said.

"I wish I could do more, Phyllis," he said blushing slightly, they spent the evening talking about how she would hide the existence of the baby from Percy, and how George had made her promise not to put his name on the birth certificate. As the war went on, he had heard of babies being born and not registered until later on when they were months old as there wasn't provision of a town hall in some places, he had heard of deaths not being registered either, things were a complete mess in England so no one would notice if she didn't register the child until later.

By this time Phyllis was three and a half months pregnant, she hoped not to have too bad a trip as she had terrible morning sickness.

"Make sure you have everything you need," he said.

"I have lots of gingersnaps," she said laughing.

"The trip might be longer than expected as sometimes the ship would stop off to pick up some poor souls that have escaped capture, its common knowledge that the Suez is well protected by the British army," he said trying to reassure her. By the end of the week, it was time to go. "Have you got everything you need?" George said, he cared immensely about Phyllis by now.

"Write to me," she whispered as they embraced.

"I'll try, I'm not one for letter writing," he said.

Phyllis gave Dora a hug. "Thank you so much for helping me, Dora, I will never forget it," she said.

"I'll write to you," Dora said, laughing.

"I'll write back," Phyllis said.

"Let me know everything that happens," Dora said waving goodbye.

Phyllis boarded the ship remembering the last time she went from Bombay to England it was with her children, this time she was totally alone. She dreaded the trip and hoped there wouldn't be fighting along the way, she settled into her cabin and fell asleep. She awoke with a start, she had dreamt that Percy found out the child she was carrying was his, she clutched her stomach and cried. "You will never have this child, I swear it," she said. Then there was a knock on her door making her jump.

"Dinner is served in the dining room, madam."

"Yes, I'm coming," she said as she sorted herself out making sure she was presentable. She went to the dining room, the company was sparce just a few passengers mostly older people, they weren't very talkative, and looked at her as though she had done something wrong. But what they were really thinking was that poor girl she looks so pale must be sea sick. Phyllis spent the rest of the trip taking food in her cabin, as she felt awkward sitting with the other passengers.

The trip went without a hitch, the ship didn't stop, it went straight through to England. Phyllis looked at the people on the dock, looking out for her father, he was standing by the car just as he was the last time she came. He was shocked when he saw her as she hadn't told her parents what had happened and didn't say that she was expecting another child.

"God, what have you done now, Phyllis, he better not come for that child, your mother and I couldn't go through that again."

"I'm sorry, Dad," Phyllis said tearfully embracing her father, "I told him it wasn't his child, he believed me, and we never have to see his face again. I've been staying at a friend's house while I was waiting for a place on the ship to England," she said.

She sat next to her father in the car, as they drove back to Surrey. Phyllis told her father what had happened and that he had tricked her into thinking the children would be coming home. She didn't mean to leave her bedroom door unlocked and by the time she realised she had been tricked he had had his way with her, it was too late. She couldn't lose another child to him so she had to devise a way of getting away with her child. She told him of the help she had, and was so grateful to George and his sister for helping her. She had sent everything to England that meant anything to her, and taken as much money as she could without being found out. Percy didn't notice she had taken the money but it was enough for Phyllis to live for a year without having to go to work, and a little extra to give to her parents for giving up a room for her.

Her father smiled, "It will be nice to have a baby in the house, it's been so long, all the children have grown up and

Pauline and Richard the youngest are away at school."

"It's not due until June, Dad, I have a few months to get sorted out, maybe we can get a maid or something to help out," she said.

"Yes, that sounds like a good idea. I'll tell Mum," he said.

They got to the house just before it got dark outside. Winifred had prepared the dinner, Jean had just come back from work, it was just the four of them, the table looked so empty, it felt so different from last time when she was at home before, Freda was there and Kitty came over often with the children. Richard was there too, but now he was away at school with Pauline, and Freda was married with a baby girl.

Winifred wanted to know everything, but Phyllis thought the less people who know the baby is Percy's the better, and decided not to say anything to her mother until Jean had gone out with her friends for the evening. Winifred was horrified "He did that to you even though you were drunk," she said really not thinking.

"Yes, Mum, but the baby's not his, it's George's," she said.

"So, the baby isn't his then?" she said puzzled.

"No not as far as anyone else knows, I cannot run the risk of him finding out, he will take it away from me and I would rather die," Phyllis said looking at her mother.

Winifred looked nonplus for a second, then it dawned on her that it was the only way Phyllis could keep her child, he would take it if he found out.

"Well, I suggest you don't talk about the baby being Percy's when we speak about it. It's George's baby, all right," she said, as though it was her idea.

Phyllis nodded, "Yes, that's right. It's George's baby."

"Drink dear?" her father said waving the whisky bottle at her.

"No, Dad, I'm expecting," she said in disbelief.

"Oh, yes, I forgot, sorry," he laughed.

"I'll make you a nice cup of cocoa," her mother said, getting up and going to the kitchen.

"Do you still have Richard's crib, Dad?" she asked.

"God no, I gave it to Freda, for Jennifer," he said. "Oh, but I think Kitty might have one though, I'll ask her tomorrow we are having luncheon with her and the children in London. Do you want to come?" he said.

"Yes, please, Dad, I can't wait to see Kitty," she replied.

Winifred came back to the lounge with the cocoa and they sat talking until they were falling asleep about how Phyllis's children looked when they visited them and what they planned to do in the future.

The next day they all went to luncheon in London and then on to the park so the children could run about while they talked about the baby and what Phyllis will do after the birth in June. Luckily Kitty had all her baby things as she did want another child, but it hadn't happened. Now they had decided not to try any longer as their lives had become quite easy as the other children got older. "Mervyn didn't want to go through the sleepless nights and nappy stage," Kitty said laughing. "You are welcome to all I have, Phil, I won't be needing them."

"Thanks," she said.

The next day Mervyn turned up with his car full of baby equipment. "Glad to be rid of them," he said. "Now we can't have another baby!" He was joking, of course, he loved his children, but they were a handful.

Phyllis had decided to give her sister Freda all her children's clothing, as she knew her child would look just like Megan or Owen, and couldn't imagine looking at it with her older children's clothing on, it would be too painful. Of course, Freda was delighted as Phyllis had impeccable taste and never bought cheap clothing for her darlings, and as Freda was also expecting, she hoped for a boy.

The toys came in useful for when the grandchildren came to Cyril and Winifred's house, they had some things to play with, and also Phyllis's child was going to live there.

Over the next few weeks Phyllis had several letters from Dora and George. George had made a plan, he was going to divorce his wife, and when he had left the army, he was going to take up a position in the Australian police force. This gave him the additional benefits of a house. He told Phyllis of how he would love it if she would go with him as his wife. Phyllis was delighted, George was a good man, not unlike her father as she came to think of it, she was stunned at the resemblance in their personalities. He was just like her father, kind, generous and funny, he would treat her child as his own, and over the coming months they had agreed that this was to be the plan.

June came and with it the much-awaited baby, a girl, she looked exactly like Megan, as Phyllis held her baby she cried, the tears flooded down her face, it was like Meg had come back to her, I won't let anyone take you my darling she said.

She named the child Priscilla June after the month she was born. Winifred loved having a baby in the house again. "She is a very quiet baby," she said to Phyllis.

Cyril butted in, "They are the ones I like!" he said laughing.

Phyllis smiled. "I'm sure she will be a good girl, just like Megan was," she said, another tear rolled down her face.

"There, there, old girl," her father said patting her on the shoulder.

"I wish Megan could see her," Phyllis said looking at her

newborn. "She is twelve now, and Owen is ten, I haven't seen them in so many years, I still ache for them." She said blowing her nose. "I thought having this baby would ease the pain but it doesn't, I think of them always, and they don't remember me," she said the tears flowing down her face

"I'm so sorry, Phil," her father said. "We were hoping that Percy would allow us to visit them by now," he said, "but he has left strict instructions that we are not to go anywhere near them. I'm guessing he's told them not to let you in either," he said.

"I know I can't see them, I phoned the school and asked if I could see them, they said he has given them instructions that I'm not to see them under any circumstances," she said. "One day the law will be changed and he won't keep me from them or I'll wait till they are of age then they will come to Australia with me and their sister," she said.

The time passed quickly. Phyllis worked at the insurance company of her old friends, the sons of the commander, her mother took care of Priscilla, and they hired a cleaner to help with the housework. George visited as often as he could, the war was at an end, but George had to stay in the army until 1949. He had applied to the police force in Australia and had been accepted, he would start in January 1950. Still, they had to get the paperwork sorted out for the journey, Phyllis had not registered Priscilla, until George came over for a visit, as he had to be present to put his name on the birth certificate, as they were not married. With the new position, he was able to travel to Australia with his family free of charge. He arranged the travel for after Christmas 1950.

Phyllis had had no contact with Megan and Owen in all the time she was there, every year she tried and every year she failed. Percy was still as cruel as ever. He had poisoned her children against her. By this time the children were sixteen and fourteen, they hadn't forgiven her for leaving them, and she couldn't convince the head of the school to let her speak to them. Every year she sent presents for the children and every year they got sent back.

It was nearing the time that they would set sail to the Australian shores, she didn't know what else to do — she looked at her daughter Priscilla playing in the garden, at least she had saved one of her children, had she known what Percy had in store for her and her children she would never have married him, she would have gone to England with her parents and had a completely different life.

This was the life she was cruelly dealt, and now she had to wave goodbye to any thoughts of reconciliation with her two older children, although it hurt her deeply, she had to do what was right for the youngest. She heard that Percy had moved to England in 1945, she hoped he would never try to contact her, anyway as far as he knew she was happily married to her new man. Phyllis had worked hard over the last few years, saving every penny for the new life George had planned for them both, she thought of her children constantly. She made one last try. She appealed to the headmistress of the school, "I'm going abroad," she said. "I won't be able to see them any other time. Please, I have a right to see them."

"I'm sorry, madam. I have strict orders from their father, he says you are not to contact them at all."

Percy had woven a web of lies to blacken Phyllis's name how she had affairs with every Tom, Dick and Harry, that he was heart-broken but he had a duty to protect his innocent children from the heartless cruel woman. And how she wouldn't know the truth if it hit her in the eye. Phyllis was running out of time, her parent told her that they wouldn't stop trying and that as soon as they were old enough, they would tell the children the truth of what happened, and why they hadn't seen or heard from their mother. They wouldn't let Percy get away with these lies he told about how Phyllis was a floozy and didn't want her children, sadly Phyllis didn't get the chance to see the children before they had to set sail for Australia, it was time to go George had been in England for the last few weeks he had spent Christmas with Phyllis's family and had bonded very well with her parents and even got to meet her cousin Cynthia alas her beloved uncle Tom had died in 1948, but her aunt Eve was spending a few days with Winifred over the Christmas period. They had experience so many deaths over the last few years her uncle Rivers died in 1938, and her beloved aunt Lilli in 1942 and her uncle Gottfried, her mother's brother, had died before this nightmare had started. Also, her father's sister, Isabelle died in 1943.

Phyllis hugged her parent's goodbye one last time. Cyril shook George's hand.

"Look after my girls, won't you, old man."

"Of course, sir," George said in reply.

"I'll write," Phyllis promised, and they wept together.

"Goodbye, my girls," Winifred said to both Phyllis and the eight-year-old Priscilla and watched as they boarded the ship bound for Australia.

The house they had been given wasn't much, but Phyllis made do, she learned to love George, and he, in turn, loved her. He had from the outset, but he could never tell Phyllis that he loved her with all his heart, and he loved the child he would raise as his own. Of course, they didn't breathe a word of the truth to her, they raised the child together, Phyllis wrote to her mother and father often, there was not a mention of cruelty or struggle.

George soon got made up to inspector, and in turn, they got a better house.

Phyllis's sister Kitty moved to Australia with her husband for two years. It was lovely to have them close, but Kitty hated it in Australia she just couldn't live without her mother and father, she missed her children who hadn't moved with them and their daughter wrote often asking when they were coming back, this gave Kitty the perfect excuse to move back to England, they moved back in 1953, Again Phyllis was alone Kitty wrote often telling her of her beautiful new house in surrey was even bigger than their mothers and fathers on Norfolk avenue, they now lived in Rickman hill surrey, and Kathy had moved in with them, For six more years they had a good life George was kind to them and Phyllis took great care of her husband and child.

She often thought of Megan and Owen especially at Christmas and on their birthdays. She kept herself busy by painting and writing letters to her siblings and parents, she loved to hear of new babies being born and all the weddings that had taken place, even her brother Henry had married his wonderful girlfriend Jane, he was teaching at a very nice school in Surrey, and Jane was a teacher too. She in turn wrote of her beautiful daughter who was growing up fast and doing very well at school. She would be soon leaving school and getting a job, at last her mother had written to her telling her she had convinced Percy to let Megan and Owen come for Christmas, Winifred had saved all the letters Phyllis has written to the children over the years and given them to Megan to read, and told the children the whole story, unfortunately the children had a hard time believing her as they thought if she loved them why is she living half way across the world now? Owen was a very polite boy and didn't say much to his grandparents about how he felt, but made no attempt to contact his mother, and Megan wanted to believe what she had been told but was very guarded. Her mother wrote telling her of Megan visiting her often, and she was trying to get her to write to her mother. Owen went from school into the army, he didn't contact his grandparents at all, and Winifred wrote of the rift between Megan and Owen. Of course, this was fuelled by Percy. He treated Megan very badly, trying to cause jealousy between the children. Megan had tried to kill herself and got thrown out of nursing college, over a nasty comment Percy had passed about taking Owen to India for Christmas, and he didn't have enough money to take her. Of course, this wasn't true, if he wanted to take them to India, he had plenty of money to do so, but he wasn't taking either of them it was just another lie. He was getting really good at lying to the children about their mother too, he didn't tell them she had been gone from his house for years, he told them that she was having a ball without them and wished never to see them again, and as he made sure that they didn't receive anything their mother had sent — they believed him.

But now Megan was visiting her grandparents; they were telling her the truth. Still, they didn't say the child she had was her full-blooded sister. Just that her mother was living in Australia with her husband and their daughter.

Megan was so jealous she couldn't see through the lies her father had told her, she was too immature to understand everything that he had said was a lie, all she thought was that her mother had replaced her and didn't love her at all, she refused to write to her mother, and that the girl was not her sister.

1961 dealt two considerable blows to Phyllis, the first her beloved father had a heart attack and died. She was devastated but didn't have the money to go to his funeral as George was sick and she was unable to leave him. George died just after Phyllis's father, she was left alone, she was able to stay for another year in the house, but then she had to find somewhere else to live. Her daughter had married a man and ran off to the other side of the country, Phyllis was totally alone and penniless. She had a small pension just enough to get by, she hated the idea of renting a room, but if that's how she was going to survive that's what she will do, she sold everything she couldn't take with her and she made a little extra money selling some of her paintings, she enjoyed painting it was just a hobby and she didn't really take it very seriously. Everyone she knew commented on how lovely her paintings were, a friend said how she loved them and as Phyllis couldn't eat the pictures, she let her have them for a small fee. In the old days she would have just given them to her friend, but now she had to be sensible, and times were harder than she had ever had. She had to apply for assistance, she took a job cleaning people's houses, but this didn't bring in much money, and at fifty-three she was embarrassed to tell anyone she cleaned houses for money. The letters she received now were of sad things Kitty wrote of her youngest son Patrick had died, she was devastated Mervyn was so sad all the time he made himself ill, and two years later he also died, it was a very sad time Phyllis remembered the lovely lively child Patrick was and the kindest boy you could ever meet, and Mervyn, her cousin, first and foremost a wonderful brother-in-law who took such great care of his family. The same year, her aunt Grace, died, her father's sister, she struggled through the next few years.

One day her daughter turned up out of the blue, she hadn't contacted her mother since George had died, Phyllis asked how she knew where she was, Priscilla said she had contacted her old friend Beula, she had all her belongings in bags and two babies in tow, her mother welcomed her in with open arms and told her they were welcome to stay with her. Priscilla had bruises on her face and was extremely emaciated and the children were thin and dirty, Phyllis proceeded to bathe them and made some soup and bread. She had learned to cook the basics as they never had the money to go out for dinner like the old days. George was a kind man, but he didn't know how to make money. The police force wages weren't high. Now he was gone, everyone was gone.

Megan had written to her mother on several occasions telling of her life. She had a son by a man who said he loved her, but when his mother wouldn't give her blessings for them to marry, he dumped her, leaving her to struggle to raise her son. She had married a man just to get housing and security for herself and her son, but he was a bully, and it ended, but not before she had two more children, girls, she at least had a house and was living on welfare. Percy gave her money for a cooker but not much more, he didn't acknowledge the girls and the boy was a bastard, so he didn't have much to do with any of them.

His son, on the other hand, Owen was still in the army and had married a wonderful woman who gave him five strong boys, he was very proud of how his son had turned out. Unfortunately, Owen wasn't in Megan's life at all and was stationed in Cyprus.

All the letters from Megan were of woe, and how badly her father treated her, Phyllis had asked Megan to come and live with her in Australia. Still, Megan was petrified of the idea, and when Phyllis had suggested she say the father of her son was dead, this gave her an excuse to turn down the offer, not that Megan could afford the travel let alone anything else. Phyllis wasn't in a position to pay for flights. Seemed like both her daughters were not very good judges of character just like she had been so many years before, Phyllis wondered how her life would be if she had stayed and accepted the life Percy had offered her, would she have seen the children and had a better life? Not a bit of struggle, to make ends meet, she often wondered.

Phyllis's days were filled with looking after the two little boys that Priscilla had dumped on her, even though she worked she went out a lot at night, one day she packed her sons up and left without so much as a by your leave. Phyllis was destroyed, it turned out the father had come to town leading Priscilla another merry dance but a few weeks later she returned all battered and torn, the children were dirty and unfed again. She promised this was it, she wouldn't leave again. Phyllis agreed to help once more, but Priscilla was pregnant just as she was when she first turned up but unfortunately, she lost the first baby.

This time she had another son, they had to apply for assistance once again, until Priscilla was able to work again, but they managed. Phyllis was supposed to get some money from Percy, he had promised her for their divorce settlement, but she never received a penny. She really did need that money but she knew he wouldn't give her anything, she left him under such terrible circumstances he didn't have a clue the child she was carrying was his, how she wished she could tell him, to see the look on his face when he found out she had kept at least one of her children would certainly kill the old blighter. But she thought of the terrible price she had paid, her children meant the world to her and she had lost them, missed all their childhood. She would never know her grandchildren, she lived so far away with no way of getting to England.

In February 1972 came the news that her loving mother had died, again Phyllis couldn't raise the money to go to England for her mother's funeral, she was very upset but by this time was used to not being able to go to her family funerals and later that year in September Percy had died she hoped that after all, she had endured he would make good on his promise to give her the money he owed her. Again, she was disappointed nothing came from him. Owen had been given his whole estate, and his sons got some cash too. Megan didn't receive a penny, and her children were also forgotten Phyllis shouldn't have been shocked, as he had never accepted Megan, she was a lowly girl, and her girls weren't anything to the curmudgeon either, this made Phyllis quite ill. She had struggled to raise his child and protect her from her birth father who was, to say the least, a cruel and disgusting excuse for a man. He had kept her away from her beloved children all their lives, he was responsible for them forgetting her, and the fact they wouldn't have anything to do with her now, she wondered what he could have possibly said to them about her, to make them deny her all those years.

The letters of encouragement she sent to Megan, were kept and read over and over again, but Megan was still very guarded. She didn't speak often to her children about their grandmother in Australia.

Phyllis had started to get letters from one of her youngest granddaughters. The child sent her photographs of herself with her older sister, unknown by her mother, she didn't get any replies, not that she didn't write, Megan had opened the letters before her daughter got home from school and didn't give them to her. As soon as the daughter had left home, she still wrote to her grandmother the letters started to arrive, Phyllis even scraped enough money together to send two teddy bears for her granddaughter's two babies, one white for the girl, one brown for the boy. Her granddaughter, was thrilled, not that they were expensive, but they were the one and the only gift she received from her grandmother whom she would never meet.

The joy was short-lived as Phyllis's life was so hard. It took its toll on her. She was dying. Her granddaughter sent some missionaries from her church to visit her. They sent her a lovely letter to say her grandmother was a wonderful character and was alert and talkative when they visited her. But alas a few weeks later she got a telegram to tell her that her grandmother had passed away, peacefully in her sleep, having never seen her children, or her grandchildren, or her great-grandchildren, all those years lost. Owen and Megan never spoke of their mother, all she had done to keep them with her, and the final straw keeping the curmudgeon away from his youngest daughter, of course, they would never know the truth of their mother's sacrifice. Priscilla kept in touch for a few years, but they lost contact when her niece moved house and Priscilla's husband Dom died.

As she was lying in the sterile room of the hospital Phyllis thought of her beloved children, and that she would soon be reunited with her parents. she wondered if they would be there on the other side. Would they all be young again? Or as they were when they passed, she couldn't wait for their arms to hold her once again. She hoped George was there too her saviour and love of her life.